「一口氣英語」

像聖經一樣，

適合各種年齡，

各種程度的人。

最新發現：

只要睡前背20分鐘不要停，

第二天早上就能夠背下來，

永遠不會忘記。

叫全班同學看著書本，

大聲一起唸，

效果奇佳。

背「一口氣英語」

要像唸經一樣，

一有空就唸，會去除煩惱，

身體健康。

當英文老師真幸運！

我上個星期去俄羅斯，看到當地的俄籍導遊，他們都是那麼興奮地在用中文介紹，嘴裡講中文講個不停，他們愈說愈興奮，因為每天都有機會練習中文，每天都在進步。

同樣地，英文老師如果上課完全用英文上，工作一定很愉快。英文課該怎麼上呢？用「一口氣英語」教英文，老師就像是一個指揮官，不需要解釋文法，不需要翻譯，只要鼓動同學不停地高聲吶喊，書中解釋很清楚，不管是翻譯或文法的說明，都有明確的交待。同學背好之後，自然而然就知道它的意思，自然知道什麼時候可以說。在班上，全班同學一起吶喊後，同學回家背就容易多了。

老師每次上課前，最好都做一次英文演講，講話的速度要慢、要有力量，儘量讓同學聽得懂。「劉毅演講式英語」中，有很多好的演講稿，可供老師選擇。想想看，每次上課，都是你練習說英文的機會，都可以用英文，和同學說人生的大道理，你每天說的英文比中文多，英文就自然流利。上課上多了，不僅會說英文，而且能講一口優美的英文，有誰能比當一個英文老師更幸運呢？每天都可以用英文發表演說，練習自己的英文口才。

「教師一口氣英語」中的 108 句，都是精挑細選，美國口語中的精華。你只要按照所背的東西來教「一口氣英語」，你就可以整堂課都用英語教書了。同樣的話講膩了，可以選擇書中的其他句子來代替，或增加一些新的句子。

　　當一個英文老師責任非常重大，學生對英文有沒有興趣，以後到底會不會說英文，這個責任完全都在老師身上。過去我們學英文的方法都錯了，美國人編的書本中的英文，美國人實際上不說，我們從課本上所學到的和美國人說的不一樣，怎麼可能會說好呢？

　　我們學跳舞，要用腳，學說英文，要用嘴，有了「一口氣英語」，只要養成自言自語的習慣，英文就會說了。讓同學唸一遍，等於看七遍，大聲唸一遍，等於小聲唸十遍，默寫一遍，也等於看七遍。所以，考試可要求同學默寫，加深印象。英文只要會說，一切都美好。有了「一口氣英語」，同學會很喜歡上課，因為立刻有效果、立刻會說英文。

　　最重要的是，如果每一回沒有背熟，沒有背到五秒鐘之內，就會忘記，背了等於白背。請老師千萬要要求同學，把每一回背到五秒鐘之內，變成直覺，就終生不會忘記。這樣日積月累下來，可不得了，台灣的老師和學生，將是全世界「一口氣英語」的先驅。

劉　毅

「教師一口氣英語」全部劇情

▶1-1　老師第一天上課，站在講台上，先用英文作為開場白：

> Listen up, class.
> Let's get started.
> Let's get to work.

▶2-1　老師叫同學跟著唸：

> Follow me.
> Repeat after me.
> Repeat exactly what I say.

▶3-1　老師叫同學大聲唸：

> Louder, please.
> Speak up, guys.
> Say it loud and clear.

▶4-1　老師叫同學看著書本大聲唸：

> Read aloud.
> Read in unison.
> Read all together as one.

▶5-1　老師叫同學不看書本背，問誰自願出來：

> Who volunteers?
> Who's first?
> You all must take a turn.

▶6-1　老師叫同學到台上來背：

> Get up here.
> Get out of your seat.
> Come on up and try.

▶7-1　老師說下課休息一下：

> Take a break.
> Take a rest.
> Everybody take five.

▶8-1　老師繼續上第二節，學生要死不活，坐在椅子上，老師說：

Look alive!
Snap to it!
Show some life.

▶9-1　老師上課，叫學生專心：

> Pay attention.
> Settle down.
> Let's behave.

▶10-1　老師叫學生默寫，學生拿著考卷在默寫：

> Write out the lesson.
> Write it from memory.
> Write it down word for word.

▶11-1　下課時間到了，老師說：

Time's up.
That's it for now.
That's all for today.

▶12-1　快下課前，老師說：

You made me proud.
You guys are the best.
I want to thank you all.

1. *Listen up, class.*

1

Listen up, class.
Let's get started.
Let's get to work.

We have lots to do.
We have no time to waste.
We're going full speed ahead.

Aim high.
Shoot for the stars.
Let's have a great class today.

---

listen up	class〔klæs, klɑs〕
get started	*get to work*
lots〔lɑts〕	ahead〔ə'hɛd〕
full speed ahead	aim〔em〕
aim high	shoot〔ʃut〕
shoot for	*shoot for the stars*

1 【內文解說】

Listen up, class.	各位同學，請注意聽。
Let's get started.	我們開始吧。
Let's get to work.	我們開始上課吧。
We have lots to do.	我們有很多東西要學。
We have no time to waste.	我們沒有時間可以浪費。
We're going full speed ahead.	我們要全速向前進。
Aim high.	要胸懷大志。
Shoot for the stars.	要有志氣。
Let's have a great class today.	我們今天好好上一堂課吧。

** ————————————————————

listen up 請注意聽　　class〔klæs, klɑs〕*n.* 班上的學生；課

get started 開始　　*get to work* 開始工作

lots〔lɑts〕*n. pl.* 許多　　ahead〔ə'hɛd〕*adv.* 向前

full speed ahead 全速向前　　aim〔em〕*v.* 瞄準

high〔haɪ〕*adv.* 高高地　　*aim high* 胸懷大志

shoot〔ʃut〕*v.* 射擊　　*shoot for* 爭取得到；為…努力

shoot for the stars 胸懷大志；有志氣（ = *reach for the stars* ）

【背景説明】

　　這九句話是老師上課的開場白。在課堂上，用
英語上課，可以更吸引同學的注意力。

1. ***Listen up***, ***class***.

　　listen up　①注意聽 (= *listen carefully*)
　　　　　　　　　②安靜一點 (= *be quiet*)

　　listen 是「聽」，up 表示「把你們的耳朵豎起來。」
　　(*Pull your ears up.*) 像貓、狗專心聽的時候，
　　都是把耳朵豎起來，所以，listen up 的主要意思就是「注意聽」。

　　class〔klæs, klɑs〕*n.* 班上的學生 (= *students in the*
　　class)；課；上課

　　　　美國老師一進到教室，最常説的話，就是：
　　Listen up, ***class***. 意思是「各位同學，請注意聽。」

　　【比較1】　Listen.（聽我説。）【在課堂上較少用】

　　　　　　　Listen up.（請注意聽。）【在課堂上較常用】

　　【比較2】　***Listen up***, ***class***.【常用】

　　　　　　　Listen up, ***students***.【劣，美國老師在課堂上
　　　　　　　　通常不説，因已有 class 來代替。校長對全校同
　　　　　　　　學發表演説，就可用 students 來稱呼學生。】

　　【比較3】　下面按照使用頻率排列：

　　　　　　　Listen up, ***class***.【最常用】
　　　　　　　（各位同學，請注意聽。）

　　　　　　　Listen up, ***everybody***.（請大家注意聽。）

　　　　　　　Listen up, ***guys***.（請大家注意聽。）
　　　　　　　　　〔gaɪz〕*n. pl.* 人

1

Listen up, ***gang***. (請大家注意聽。)
〔gæŋ〕*n.* 群

gang 多指「幫派」，現在也指「一群人」(= *a group of people*)，和 guys 或 everybody 意義相同，表示「大家」或「每一個人」。

Listen up, ***you guys***. (請你們注意聽。)

Listen up, ***ladies and gentlemen***.【適用於高中以上】
(各位先生、各位女士，請注意聽。)

Listen up, ***boys and girls***.【適用於中小學生】
(孩子們，請注意聽。)

Listen up, ***people***. (請大家注意聽。)【適用於高中以上】

【比較4】 凡是 ***Listen up*** 後面有 class 或 everybody
之類的字，美國人就不習慣再加 please。這
和中國人的思想有點不同。

中文： 各位同學，請注意聽。

英文： ***Listen up***, *class*.【正】
Please listen up, *class*.【文法正確，
美國人少說】
Please listen up.【正】
Listen up, *class*, *please*.【文法正確，
美國人不說】

【比較5】 美國老師上課前，除了說 ***Listen up***, *class*.
之外，也說些其他的話：

Listen up, *class*. (各位同學，請注意聽。)【最常用】
= Attention, please. (請注意聽。)【第二常用】
= I'd like your attention.【第五常用】
(我要你們注意聽。)【attention〔ə'tɛnʃən〕*n.* 注意力】

1

= May I have your attention, please?【第三常用】
　（請注意聽，好嗎？）

= Can I have your attention, please?【第六常用】
　（請注意聽，好嗎？）

= Give me your attention, please.【第七常用】
　（請注意聽。）

= Give me your attention, everybody.【第八常用】
　（大家請注意聽。）

= I want your attention, please.【第四常用】
　（我要請你們注意聽。）

2. *Let's get started.*

　　這句話是一個慣用句，在文法上無法解釋，為
什麼用被動，是固定用法。字面的意思是「讓我們
被開始。」事實上，意思是「我們開始吧。」

【比較1】 *Let's get started.*【正】
　　　　 Let's get begun.【誤】

【比較2】 Let's start.【正】
　　　　 Let's begin.【正】

　　　　這兩句話都常用，但是美國人更習慣在 start
後面，加一些字詞。如：

　　　　Let's start right now.（我們現在開始吧。）
　　　　Let's start working.（我們開始工作吧。）
　　　　Let's start doing our homework.
　　　　　（我們開始寫作業吧。）

　　　　begin 後面雖然也可以接字詞，但是用法沒有
start 來得普遍。

1

【比較3】 下面的句子意思相同，都是美國人常說
的話，我們按照使用的頻率排列：

中文： 我們開始吧。

英文：

> *Let's get started.*【最常用】
> = Let's rock and roll.【第二常用】
> = Let's start the show.【第三常用】

> = Let's get the ball rolling.
> = Let's get the show on the road.
> = Let's get going.

> = Let's get to it.
> = Let's get at it.
> = Let's get on it.

> = Let's roll.
> = Let's begin.
> = Let's start.

> *rock and roll* 開始　　*start the show* 開始
> *get the ball rolling* 開始進行
> *get the show on the road* 著手工作；開始活動
> *get going* 開始
> *get to* 開始；著手處理 (= *get at* = *get on*)
> roll〔rol〕*v.* 開始

3. *Let's get to work.*

   get to work 開始工作

   > *get to* 原本的意思是「到達」，像 When did
   you *get to* school today? (你今天幾點到達學校？)。
   Let's get to work. 中的 work 是名詞，這句話的字面
   意思是「我們到達工作吧。」引申為「我們開始工作吧。」
   (= *Let's start working.*)

1

　　字典上還沒有 ***get to work*** 這個成語，但美國人常說。例如：Let's stop talking and get to work. （我們不要講話，開始工作吧。）

　　在課堂上，老師說：***Let's get to work.*** 意思就是「我們開始上課吧。」

【比較】 下面是美國人常說的話，我們按照使用頻率
　　　　 排列：

中文： 我們開始工作吧。

英文： ***Let's get to work.*** 【第一常用】
　　　 Let's get down to business. 【第二常用】
　　　 Let's get down to work. 【第三常用】

　　　 Let's start working.
　　　 Let's start doing our work.
　　　 Let's do what needs to be done.

　　　 Let's get serious.
　　　 Let's get to the task at hand.
　　　 Let's knuckle down.

get down to business 著手工作 (= *get down to work*)
get to 開始　　serious (ˈsɪrɪəs) *adj.* 認真的
task (tæsk) *n.* 工作　　***at hand*** 在手邊
knuckle (ˈnʌkḷ) *n.* 手指的關節　*v.* 用拳頭敲
knuckle down 認真地著手工作

1

4. *We have lots to do.*

lots〔lɑts〕*n. pl.* 許多；許多東西

> 這句話源自：We have lots *of work* to do. 意思是「我們有很多事要做。」在上課的時候，老師說這句話，意思就是「我們有很多東西要學。」等於 We have lots to learn.

> *lots* 和 *a lot* 意義相同，使用頻率也相同。

> We have *lots* to do. (我們有很多事要做。)
> = We have *a lot* to do.

> 美國人常用 tons 來代替 lots 或 a lot。

> We have tons to do. (我們有很多事要做。)
> 　　　　　〔tʌnz〕*n. pl.* 許多
> = We have tons of work to do.

【比較】下面四句意思相同，都表示「我們有很多事要做。」

> *We have lots to do.*【較常用】
> We have lots of work to do.【常用】

> *We have a lot to do.*【較常用】
> We have a lot of work to do.【常用】

美國老師在課堂上也常說：

> We're going to be busy today. (我們今天會很忙。)
> We have a lot to cover today.
> (我們今天要上很多課。)【cover〔'kʌvə〕*v.* 覆蓋；討論】

> We have much to do. (我們有很多事要做。)
> We have many things to do. (我們有很多事要做。)

1

5. *We have no time to waste.*

waste〔west〕v. 浪費

這句話的意思是「我們沒有時間可以浪費。」
也可以説成：We have no time to relax. (我們
沒有時間輕鬆。)〔rɪ'læks〕v. 放鬆

【比較】We have no time to waste.【正】
We have no time to be wasted.【誤】
【當形容詞用的不定詞片語，通常用主動語態。
(詳見「文法寶典」p.424)】

We have no time to spare.【正】
(我們沒有時間剩下。)〔spɛr〕v. 騰出；剩下
We have no time to be spared.【誤】

美國小孩子常喜歡説：We have no time to
play. (我們沒有時間玩。) 在課堂上，老師當然
不會説這句話。

6. *We're going full speed ahead.*

(at) full speed 儘快地；以最快速度地；拼命地
ahead〔ə'hɛd〕adv. 向前
full speed ahead 全速往前 (= *as fast as possible*)

這句話的意思是「我們要全速向前進。」
full speed ahead 源自海軍用語。

1

【比較】 full speed ahead 已經是一個成語，
有了 ahead，前面不可加 at。

We're going *full speed ahead*. 【正】
(我們要全速向前進。)
We're going *at full speed ahead*. 【誤】

We're going *full speed*. 【正】
(我們將以最快速度進行。)
We're going *at full speed*. 【正】
(我們將以最快速度進行。)

在所有中外字典上都找不到 full speed ahead，
除了四千多頁的「東華英漢辭典」，這個好的成語，
我們一定要學會使用。

full speed ahead 往往和 go 連用，是因為美
國人常說 go ahead (向前進行)，自然就會習慣說
出 ___go full speed ahead___。

【例】 The deadline is one week away. We must
go full speed ahead.
(截止期限只剩一星期。我們必須以最快的
速度進行。)
【deadline〔'dɛd,laɪn〕*n.* 截止期限
away〔ə'we〕*adv.* (用在名詞後面) 隔開…遠；尚有…時間】

If you want to speak English well, you
must *go full speed ahead*.
(如果你想把英文說好，就必須盡全力。)

You should *go full speed ahead* to finish
the job. (你應該儘快完成這個工作。)

1

7. *Aim high*.

aim〔em〕*v.* 瞄準　　high〔haɪ〕*adv.* 高高地

　　aim high 的字面意思是「向高處瞄準」，引申爲「胸懷大志」。美國的父母常常鼓勵小孩：

No matter what you do, *aim high*,
and try your best.
（無論你做什麼事，都要胸懷大志，盡力而爲。）

8. *Shoot for the stars*.

shoot〔ʃut〕*v.* 射擊

shoot for 爭取得到（或完成）；爲⋯而努力

Shoot for the stars.

　　這句話字面的意思是「要向星星射擊。」引申爲「要胸懷大志；要有志氣。」在美國，有些學校把 *Shoot for the stars.* 寫在牆上，來鼓勵同學。在畢業典禮的時候，校長也常用這句話，來勉勵畢業生。

【比較】

　　Shoot for the stars. (要胸懷大志。)【最常用】
　　【在所有的字典上找不到，但美國人常說。】

　　Shoot for the sky. (要胸懷大志。)
　　【NTC's Dictionary of American Slang 中有，但美國人較少說。】

　　Shoot for the moon. (要胸懷大志。)
　　【Talking American Dictionary 中有，但美國人少說。】

　　Shoot for the top. (要胸懷大志。)【常用】

以上四句中的 Shoot，都可用 Reach 代替。

1

【例1】 Don't accept mediocrity. ***Shoot for the stars.***
〔ˌmidɪˈɑkrətɪ〕 *n.* 平凡；平庸

(不要接受平庸。要胸懷大志。)

【例2】 ***Shoot for the stars.*** Don't settle for second best.

(要有志氣。不要退而求其次。)

【***settle for*** 勉強接受　***second best*** 第二好的】

【例3】 Dream big dreams. ***Shoot for the stars.***

(要有偉大的夢想。要胸懷大志。)

Shoot for the stars. 也可説成 Reach for the stars.

9. ***Let's have a great class today.***

class〔klæs,klɑs〕*n.* 課；上課；全班同學

【比較】 下面是美國老師在課堂上常説的話，我們
按照使用頻率排列：

中文： 我們今天好好上一堂課吧。

英文： ***Let's have a great class today.***【最常用】

Let's have a good class today.

Let's have an excellent class today.

Let's have a super class today.
〔ˈsupɚ〕*adj.* 極好的

Let's have a wonderful class today.

Let's have a productive class today.
〔prəˈdʌktɪv〕*adj.* 有生產力的；有收穫的

【對話練習 1】

1

A：Listen up, class.

B：We're quiet.
We're listening.
You have our attention.

A：Let's get started.

B：Yeah, let's start.
It's time to start.
It's time for class.
【yeah〔jɛ〕*adv.* 是；可以（= *yes*）】

A：Let's get to work.

B：Yeah, it's time to work.
Let's get serious.
Let's get down to business.

A：We have lots to do.

B：Don't tell me.

I already know that.
It's going to be a busy day.

A：各位同學，請注意聽。

B：我們很安靜。
我們正在聽。
我們在專心聽。

A：我們開始吧。

B：好，我們開始。
是該開始的時候了。
是該上課的時候了。

A：我們開始工作吧。

B：是啊，是該工作的時候了。
我們辦正事吧。
我們開始辦正事吧。

A：我們有很多事要做。

B：不必告訴我。(暗示「我已
經知道了。」)
我已經知道了。
今天會很忙碌。

1 【對話練習 2】

A： We have no time to waste.

B： Don't remind me.
〔 rɪ'maɪnd 〕 *v.* 提醒

I have so much to do.

I wish I had more time.

A： We're going full speed ahead.

B： I can handle it.
〔'hændḷ 〕 *v.* 應付；處理

I'm ready for the challenge.

That's the way I like it.
【challenge 〔'tʃælɪndʒ 〕 *n.* 挑戰】

A： Aim high.

B： I always aim high.

I try to reach for the sky.

I have big plans for the future.
【*reach for the sky* 胸懷大志】

A： Shoot for the stars.

B： I always shoot for the top.

I dream big dreams.

I want to achieve my potential.

【*shoot for the top* 胸懷大志　　achieve 〔 ə'tʃiv 〕 *v.* 達到
potential 〔 pə'tɛnʃəl 〕 *n.* 潛力】

A： 我們沒有時間可以浪費。

B： 不必提醒我。(暗示「我
已經知道了。」)
我有很多事要做。
真希望我有更多的時間。

A： 我們要全速向前進。

B： 我可以應付。

我準備好要接受挑戰。
我喜歡那樣。

A： 要胸懷大志。

B： 我總是胸懷大志。
我很努力要胸懷大志。
我對未來有遠大的計劃。

A： 要胸懷大志；要有志氣。

B： 我總是胸懷大志。
我有偉大的夢想。
我想要發揮自己的潛力。

2. Follow me.

2

Follow me.
Repeat after me.
Repeat exactly what I say.

Say what I say.
Do what I do.
All eyes on me.

Raise your hand.
Make a fist.
Sound off after me.

---

follow〔'falo〕　　　　　repeat〔rɪ'pit〕
exactly〔ɪg'zæktlɪ〕　　raise〔rez〕
fist〔fɪst〕　　　　　　*sound off*

【內文解說】

2

Follow me.　　　　　　　　　跟著我說。
Repeat after me.　　　　　　跟著我唸。
Repeat exactly what I say.　　請完全按照我的話說。

Say what I say.　　　　　　　跟著我說。
Do what I do.　　　　　　　　照我的手勢做。
All eyes on me.　　　　　　　請大家眼睛看著我。

Raise your hand.　　　　　　　把你的手舉起來。
Make a fist.　　　　　　　　　握緊拳頭。
Sound off after me.　　　　　　跟我大聲喊。

** ─────────────────────

follow〔'falo〕*v.* 跟隨；仿效
repeat〔rɪ'pit〕*v.* 重複；重說；跟著唸
exactly〔ɪg'zæktlɪ〕*adv.* 完全地；確實地；精確地
raise〔rez〕*v.* 舉起　　　fist〔fɪst〕*n.* 拳頭
sound off 大聲喊

2

【背景説明】

這一回的重點，是上課的時候，老師叫同學跟著唸。「一口氣英語」的精神所在，就是讓同學上課時，不停地唸，不停地喊。

1. *Follow me.*

follow〔'falo〕v. 跟隨；仿效

這句話的主要意思是「跟著我走。」(= *Follow in my footsteps.*) 但是，在教室裡面，這句話的意思是「跟著我說。」(= *Say what I say.*) 有些美國老師習慣先說：Listen carefully.（仔細聽。）再接著說 ***Follow me.***

2. *Repeat after me.*

repeat〔rɪ'pit〕v. 重複；重說；跟著唸

這句話的意思是「跟著我唸。」或「跟著我說。」

【比較】中文： 跟著我說。

英文： ***Repeat after me.***【正】
Say it after me.【正】
Speak after me.【誤】
Talk after me.【誤】

speak 是「說話」，talk 是「談話」，你不可能說「跟著我說話。」或「跟著我談話。」

2

3. *Repeat exactly what I say.*

   exactly〔ɪgˈzæktlɪ〕*adv.* 完全地；確實地；精確地

   【比較1】 Repeat what I say.【正，常用】
   　　　　　【repeat 在此是及物動詞】
   　　　　　Repeat after what I say.【誤，文法上正確，
   　　　　　但美國人不說，因爲這句話美國人已經習慣簡
   　　　　　化，能省就省。】

   【比較2】 *Repeat exactly what I say.*【常用，加強語氣】
   　　　　　（請完全照著我的話說。）
   　　　　　Repeat what I say.【常用，一般語氣】
   　　　　　（請跟著我說。）

4. *Say what I say.*

   　　這句話字面的意思是「說我所說的話。」引申
   爲「跟著我說。」也可說成：

   Please say what I say.（請跟著我說。）
   Say *exactly* what I say.（確實跟著我說。）
   Please say *exactly* what I say.
   （請確實跟著我說。）

2

5. ***Do what I do****.*

　　這句話字面的意思是「做我所做的事。」在課堂上的意思就是「照我的手勢做。」也可以加強語氣說成：

Do whatever I do. (我做什麼，你們就做什麼。)
Follow whatever I do. (我做什麼，你們就跟著做。)
Follow my every move. (模仿我的每個動作。)
　　　　　　　　　〔 muv 〕*n.* 動作；移動

也有美國老師說：

Imitate me. (模仿我。)
〔'ɪmə͵tet 〕*v.* 模仿
Imitate my actions. (模仿我的動作。)
Imitate what I do. (模仿我的動作。)

　　上面三個句子中的 Imitate，都可用 Mimic
〔'mɪmɪk 〕*v.* 模仿 取代。像：Mimic me.
Mimic my actions. Mimic what I do. 意思
都是和上面三句一樣。

6. ***All eyes on me****.*

　　這句話源自：I want all eyes on me. 字面的意思是「我要你們的眼睛，全部在我身上。」引申為「請大家眼睛看著我。」

　　通常老師站在前面，叫同學跟著唸的時候，都會叫他們不要看課本，這樣子他們才會專心聽。

美國老師常說：

> Don't look at your books. (不要看書本。)
> ***All eyes on me***. (眼睛看著我。)
> I want your attention. (我要你們注意聽。)
> 〔ə'tɛnʃən〕 *n.* 注意

美國老師在監考的時候，常說：

> ***All eyes on your papers***. (眼睛看著考卷。)
> 【用 papers，因句中有 All。】
> Don't look around. (不要東張西望。)
> No looking at your book. (不准看書。)
> 【*No + V-ing* 表「禁止～」。】
> 中國人說：「不要偷看書。」而美國人的思想
> 是「不要看書；不准看書。」

下面三句話，意義都相同，都表示「請大家眼睛
看著我。」有時也含有「請大家注意聽。」的意思。

> ***All eyes on me***.
> = I want all eyes on me.
> = I want everyone to look at me.

7. *Raise your hand.*

raise 〔rez〕 *v.* 舉起

這句話的意思是「把你的手舉起來。」

【比較】 ***Raise your hand***. (把你的手舉起來。)
　　　　【針對一個人或全體】
　　　　Raise your hands. (把你們的手舉起來。)
　　　　【針對全體】

2

　　在課堂上，老師除了說 ***Raise your hand.*** 以外，還常說：Put your hand up. 或 Put your hands up. 都表示「把手舉起來。」【*put up* 舉起】

【比較】***Raise your hand.***【一般語氣】

　　　　Put them up.【命令語氣】

　　　　Put them up. 說快就變成 Put 'em up. 通常是老師說完 Raise your hand. 後，再加強語氣說 Put them up.。

　　很奇怪，美國人說 Put your hand up. 卻不說 *Put it up.*（誤）可能源自警察用語：

　　　　Freeze!（不准動！）

　　　　Put them up!（把手舉起來！）

　　　　【此時 them 是指 your hands】

　　叫同學把手舉高，可以說 ***Raise your hand in the air.***【*in the air* 在空中】

　　也有美國人說 Raise your arm. 字面的意思是「把手臂舉起來。」引申為「把手舉高。」

【比較】　下面兩句話，意思都是「把手舉起來。」

Raise your hand.

　　【手舉得高或不高均可，
　　　像圖 1 或圖 2。】

【圖 1】

Raise your arm.

　　【手舉得很高，如圖 2。
　　　這句話中國人思想中
　　　沒有。】

【圖 2】

2

8. ***Make a fist***.

fist〔fɪst〕*n.* 拳頭

這句話的意思是「握緊拳頭。」在所有的字典上,「握緊拳頭。」都是 *Clench your fist.*【劣】,
〔klɛntʃ〕*v.* 握緊
但事實上,美國人都說 Make a fist. 或説:
Clench your fingers to make a fist.（把拳頭握緊。）【字面的意思是「把你的手指握緊,成爲拳頭。」】

9. ***Sound off after me***.

sound off 大聲喊

這句話的意思是「跟我大聲喊。」或「跟我呼口號。」源自美國軍隊裡面,呼口號前所説的話。

【比較】 中文: 跟我大聲喊。

英文: ***Sound off after me.***【最常用】

Shout out after me.【最常用】

Yell out after me.【較常用】

Repeat loudly after me.【常用】

【***sound off*** 大聲喊（= *shout out* = *yell out*）
loudly〔'laʊdlɪ〕*adv.* 大聲地】

【對話練習 1】

A：Follow me.

B：No problem.
　　I will.
　　I will follow you.

A：Repeat after me.

B：Sure thing.
　　I understand.
　　I'll repeat after you.
　　【*sure thing* 當然；沒問題】

A：Repeat exactly what I say.

B：I'll try.
　　I'll do my best.
　　I'll do the best I can.

A：Say what I say.

B：I can do that.
　　I'll mimic you.
　　I'll repeat what you say.

A：跟著我說。

B：沒問題。
　　我會。
　　我會跟著你說。

A：跟著我唸。

B：沒問題。
　　我知道。
　　我會跟著你唸。

A：請完全照著我的話說。

B：我會試試看。
　　我會盡力。
　　我會盡力。

A：跟著我說。

B：我可以那麼做。
　　我會模仿你。
　　我會跟著你說。

2

【對話練習 2】

A : Do what I do.

B : OK, I'll try.
   I'll give it a shot.
   I'll try to copy what you do.
   【*give it a shot* 試試看
   copy〔'kɑpɪ〕*v.* 模仿】

A : All eyes on me.

B : You have everyone's attention.
   We're all looking at you.
   We're paying attention to you.

A : Raise your hand.

B : My hand is up.
   I feel a little silly.
   Tell me what to do.
   【silly〔'sɪlɪ〕*adj.* 愚蠢的】

A : Sound off after me.

B : I'm ready.
   I'll follow your lead.
   I'm ready to follow you.
   【*follow one's lead* 以~為榜樣】

A : 照我的手勢做。

B : 好的，我會試試看。
   我會試試看。
   我會試著模仿你的手勢。

A : 請大家眼睛看著我。

B : 大家都很專心。

   我們都在看著你。
   我們都在注意你。

A : 把手舉起來。

B : 我的手舉起來了。
   我覺得有點呆。
   告訴我該怎麼做。

A : 跟我大聲喊。

B : 我準備好了。
   我會以你為榜樣。
   我準備好要跟你一起喊了。

3. Louder, please.

Louder, please.
Speak up, guys.
Say it loud and clear.

Raise your voices.
I can't hear you.
Don't sound like zombies.

Turn it up.
Shout it out!
Tell it to the world!

---

loud〔laʊd〕
guy〔gaɪ〕
raise〔rez〕
sound〔saʊnd〕
turn up

speak up
loud and clear
voice〔vɔɪs〕
zombie〔'zɑmbɪ〕
shout out

【內文解說】

Louder, please.	請大聲一點。
Speak up, guys.	你們說大聲一點，不要怕。
Say it loud and clear.	說大聲一點、清楚一點。
Raise your voices.	提高你們的聲音。
I can't hear you.	我聽不到你們的聲音。
Don't sound like zombies.	聲音不要像蚊子叫一樣。
Turn it up.	說話大聲一點。
Shout it out!	大聲喊！
Tell it to the world!	大聲說出來，讓大家都聽到！

** ——————————————————

loud〔laud〕*adv.* 大聲地
speak up 大聲說；大膽說　　guy〔gaɪ〕*n.* 人
loud and clear 大聲又清楚；非常清楚地
raise〔rez〕*v.* 提高　　voice〔vɔɪs〕*n.* 聲音
sound〔saund〕*v.* 聽起來　　zombie〔'zɑmbɪ〕*n.* 僵屍
turn up 開大聲；把（音量）調大
shout out 大聲說出；大聲喊出

【背景說明】

　　一般中國學生在課堂上，都很害羞，不喜歡講話，老師可用這九句話，來鼓勵同學大聲說。

3

1. *Louder, please.*
   loud〔laʊd〕*adv.* 大聲地

　　這句話的意思是「請大聲一點。」老師也常說成：Everybody, louder, please.（請大家大聲一點。）這句話源自：Speak louder, please.（請說大聲一點。）或 Say it louder, please.（請說大聲一點。）

2. *Speak up, guys.*
   speak up ①大聲說（ = *speak loud enough to be heard* ）
   　　　　　　②大膽說（ = *speak without fear or hesitation* ）
   guy〔gaɪ〕*n.* 人；傢伙

　　這句話的意思是「你們說大聲一點，不要怕。」guys 等於 you guys。凡是對一群男女，可以說 guys 或 you guys，對單獨一群男生，或是一群女生，也可以說 guys 或 you guys，只有單獨一個女生，不能說 *guy* 或 *you guy*。guy 單數的時候，是指一個男人（ = *a man* ）。

3

　　在課堂上，稱呼同學，除了用 guys、you guys 以外，還可以用 class、boys and girls 等。(詳見第一回)

　　下面兩個比較，說明 speak up 的兩個意思：

【比較1】 ***Speak up***. (大聲說。)【最常用】
　　　　　= Speak louder. (說大聲一點。)【第二常用】
　　　　　= Say it louder. (說大聲一點。)【第三常用】
　　　　　= Speak clearly. (說清楚。)【第四常用】

【比較2】 ***Speak up***. (大膽地說出來。)【最常用】
　　　　　= Say it. (說出來。)【第二常用】
　　　　　= Just say it. (說出來吧。)【第三常用】

　　　　　= Don't hold it in. (不要忍住不說。)
　　　　　= Don't keep it in. (不要憋著不說。)
　　　　　= Don't be silent. (不要不出聲音。)

【***hold in*** 忍耐；壓抑 (= *keep in*)
silent (ˈsaɪlənt) *adj.* 無聲的 】

3. ***Say it loud and clear***.

loud and clear ①大聲又清楚
　　　　　　　　②非常清楚地 (= *clearly and distinctly*)

　　loud and clear 源自早期無線電接收人員說的話。通常發報員會說："Do you hear me?" (你有沒有聽到我的聲音？) 接收員回答："Yes, ***loud and clear***." (有，很清楚。) 或"I hear you ***loud and clear***." (我聽得很清楚。)

3

Say it loud and clear. 在這裡的意思是「說大聲一點、清楚一點。」

【比較】*Say it loud and clear*. 【正】
　　　　Say it loudly and clearly. 【劣，文法上正確，但美國人少説】

　　文法上，雖然 loudly 和 clearly 可以當副詞用，但是因爲已經有 *loud and clear* 這種慣用語，所以，美國人不習慣説 *loudly and clearly*，但是可以説：Say it loudly. 或 Say it clearly.

　　loud and clear 到底是「清楚地」呢？還是「大聲又清楚地」呢？要看實際情況而定。在教室裡面，老師如果説 *Say it loud and clear*. 就是叫你「說話大聲，發音也要清楚。」

　　美國人還常説：*I can read you loud and clear*. 這句話的意思有兩個：
①我聽得很清楚。(= *I can hear you loud and clear*.)
②我完全了解。(= *I totally understand*.)

4. *Raise your voices*.
raise〔rez〕*v*. 提高　　voice〔vɔɪs〕*n*. 聲音

　　這句話的意思是「提高你們的聲音。」引申爲「大聲一點。」也可以加強語氣説成：I want you all to raise your voices. (我要你們全體都大聲一點。)

【比較】Raise your voices. 【正】
　　　　Raise your sound. 【誤，sound 通常是指機器或東西發出來的聲音。】

3

5. *I can't hear you.*

hear〔hɪr〕*v.* 聽到

　　　這句話源自 *I can't hear you* very well. (正)
意思是「我聽不清楚你們講的話。」在教室裡，老
師喜歡說這句話，叫同學大聲說出來，並非老師
聽不清楚學生說的話。

　　　美國軍隊裡的隊長，明明已經聽到隊員在喊，
還是會不斷地喊著：*I can't hear you.* 因為他想要
藉由大聲喊口號，來激勵士氣。

　　下面都是老師在課堂上常說的話：

Speak up. *I can't hear you.*

（說大聲一點。我聽不清楚。）

Louder, please. *I can't hear you.*

（請大聲一點。我聽不清楚你們的聲音。）

I can't hear you. Please say that again.

（我聽不清楚。請你們再說一遍。）

What did you say? *I can't hear you.*

（你們說什麼？我聽不清楚。）

You guys are not loud enough. *I can't
hear you.*

（你們不夠大聲。我聽不清楚你們的聲音。）

Your voices are too low. *I can't hear you.*

（你們的聲音太小。我聽不清楚你們的聲音。）

6. *Don't sound like zombies.*

sound〔saʊnd〕*v.* 聽起來

zombie〔ˈzɑmbɪ〕*n.* 僵屍（= *a walking dead person*）

　　zombie 這個字，主要的意思是「僵屍」，但是一般英漢字典都沒有說明清楚。

　　這句話字面的意思是「不要聽起來像僵屍。」在此引申為「聲音不要像蚊子叫一樣。」可能是因為死去的人不會說話。

【比較】　中外文化思想不同，很多句子都不能直接翻譯。

中文：　你的聲音像蚊子叫。

英文：　*You sound like a mosquito buzzing.*
　　　　【文法正確，但美國人不作此比喻。】
　　　　You sound like a zombie.【正，常用】
　　　　You sound like you're dead.【正，常用】
　　　　You sound like you're dying.【正，常用】

　　美國人常常自我幽默，早上如果精神不好，他會說：Do I look like a zombie today?（我今天看起來有沒有像僵屍？）或 I feel like a zombie today.（我今天覺得自己像僵屍。）或 Am I acting like a zombie?（我是不是樣子像僵屍？）
〔ˈæktɪŋ〕*v.* 行動；舉止

3

美國人習慣把下列的人用 zombie（僵屍）來
比喻：①奇怪的人（a weird person）
〔wɪrd〕*adj.* 奇怪的
②很愚笨的人（a very stupid person）
③很疲倦的人（a very tired person）
④有毒癮的人（a drug addict）
〔'ædɪkt〕*n.* 上癮的人

所以，美國人看到喝醉酒的人或衣著奇怪的人，他
們會說：He looks like a zombie.（他看起來像僵屍。）

7. ***Turn it up.***

turn up 開大聲；把（音量）調大

這句話源自 Turn up the volume.（把音量
〔'vɑljəm〕*n.* 音量
調大。）turn up 是「調大」的意思，像：Could
you please turn up the TV?（能不能請你把電
視的音量調大？）Please turn up the radio.
（請把收音機的聲音調大。）

Turn it up. 的字面意思是
「把它調大。」it 是指「音量」，
所以引申為：①把音量調大。
②說話大聲一點。

【比較】
中文：　聲音調大一點。
英文：　***Turn it up.***【最常用】
Turn up the volume.【較常用】
Turn the volume up.【正，常用】
Turn up it.【誤，碰到代名詞，turn up 必須分開。】

3

　　turn up 的主要意思是「把（音量）調大」，「調小聲」就是 turn down。像 Please turn the radio down.（請把收音機的聲音調小。）但是叫別人説話小聲一點，卻不能説 *Turn it down.*（把它關小聲。）只能説 Keep it down.（小聲一點。）（= *Lower your voice.*）

8. *Shout it out!*

shout〔ʃaut〕*v.* 叫；大聲喊
shout out　大聲説出；大聲喊出

　　這句話字面的意思是「把它大聲說出來！」引申為「大聲喊！」。

【比較】下面三句話意思相同，但語氣不同。

　　　Shout it!（大聲説！）【一般語氣】
　　　Shout it out!（大聲喊出！）【加強語氣】
　　　Shout it out loud!（拼命大聲喊出！）【語氣最強】
　　　　　　〔laud〕*adv.* 大聲地

【例】 Don't say it. Shout it!
　　　（不要只是説。要大聲喊！）
　　　Don't hold back. *Shout it out!*
　　　（不要猶豫不決。大聲喊出來！）
　　　【*hold back* 猶豫不決（= *hesitate*）】
　　　Don't just yell it. Shout it out loud!
　　　（不要只是喊。要拼命大聲喊出來！）

9. *Tell it to the world!*

這句話美國人常説，但是字典上找不到，它的字面意思是「告訴全世界這件事！」引申爲「讓全世界聽到！」也就是「大聲說出來，讓大家都聽到！」(= *Say it so loudly that everyone can hear you!*)

這句話是比喻用法，有誇張的意味。下面六句話意義相同：

Tell it to the world!【第一常用】
Let everyone hear you!【第二常用】
Let the whole world hear you!【第三常用】

Let the whole building hear you!【第四常用】
Tell it to everybody!【第五常用】
Tell it to the whole world!【第六常用】

在學校裡面上課，老師還可以説：Tell it to the whole school! 意思也是「大聲說出來，讓大家都聽到！」當哪一個人說話太小聲，老師會説：Tell it to the whole class! 意思是「說大聲一點，讓全班聽到！」。

【對話練習 1】

3

A： Louder, please.

B： No problem.
How's this?
Is this okay?

A： 請大聲一點。

B： 沒問題。
這樣如何？
這樣可以嗎？

A： Speak up, guys.

B： Sure thing.
We can do that.
Whatever you say.
【*sure thing* 當然；可以】

A： 你們說大聲一點，不要怕。

B： 當然可以。
我們做得到。
悉聽尊便。

A： Say it loud and clear.

B： I understand.
I'll be loud.
I'll say it as clearly as I can.

A： 說大聲一點、清楚一點。

B： 我了解。
我會大聲。
我會儘量說清楚。

A： Raise your voices.

B： No problem at all.
We'll speak up.
We'll speak louder.

A： 提高你們的聲音。

B： 沒問題。
我們會大聲說。
我們會說大聲一點。

【對話練習 2】

A：I can't hear you.

B：Sorry about that.
　　I didn't know.
　　Thanks for telling me.

A：Turn it up.

B：You got it.
　　Anything for you.
　　Your wish is my command.
　　【command〔kə'mænd〕*n.* 命令】

A：Shout it out!

B：Get ready.
　　Be prepared.
　　I'm really going to do it.

A：Tell it to the world!

B：Great idea.
　　Everyone should know.
　　Everyone should hear
　　about this.

A：我聽不到你的聲音。

B：很抱歉。
　　我不知道。
　　謝謝你告訴我。

A：說話大聲一點。

B：沒問題。
　　我願意為你做任何事。
　　我聽你的吩咐。

A：大聲喊！

B：準備好。
　　你要做好準備。
　　我真的要喊了。

A：大聲說出來，讓大家都
　　聽到！

B：好主意。
　　大家都應該知道。
　　大家都應該聽到這件事。

4. *Read aloud.*

Read aloud.
Read in unison.
Read all together as one.

I'll say the first line.
You repeat and continue.
Go on and on nonstop.

Don't let up.
Keep at it!
Keep going no matter what.

---

aloud (ə'laʊd)	unison ('junəsn̩)
in unison	*all together*
as one	line (laɪn)
repeat (rɪ'pit)	continue (kən'tɪnju)
on and on	nonstop ('nɑn'stɑp)
let up	*keep at*
Keep at it!	*keep + V-ing*

【內文解說】

Read aloud.	唸出聲音來。
Read in unison.	一起唸。
Read all together as one.	全體一起唸。
I'll say the first line.	我將唸第一行。
You repeat and continue.	你們重覆，並且往下繼續唸。
Go on and on nonstop.	繼續不要停。
Don't let up.	不要停止。
Keep at it!	堅持下去！
Keep going no matter what.	無論如何都要繼續唸。

** ────────────────────

aloud〔ə'laʊd〕*adv.* 出聲地
unison〔'junəsn̩〕*n.* 和諧；一致　　***in unison*** 同時地；一起
all together 一起　　***as one*** 一致地
line〔laɪn〕*n.* 行　　repeat〔rɪ'pit〕*v.* 重複；重說
continue〔kən'tɪnju〕*v.* 繼續
on and on 繼續不斷地；一直不停地
nonstop〔'nɑn'stɑp〕*adv.* 不斷地；不停地
let up 停止　　***keep at*** 繼續做
Keep at it! 繼續做下去！；堅持下去！　　***keep* + *V-ing*** 繼續

【背景説明】

　　　背「一口氣英語」最簡單的方法，就是讓全班同學一起看著書本唸，連續唸十到二十分鐘不要停，就可以背下來了。老師可用這九句話，來指揮同學唸。

4

1. *Read aloud*.

aloud〔ə'laʊd〕*adv.* ①出聲地 (= *out loud*)

　　②大聲地 (= *loudly*)【作「大聲地」解，是古語用法，現在不用】

這句話的意思是「唸出聲音來。」

【比較 1】

　　① 默唸。Read quietly. 或 Read silently.
　　　　　　或 Read to yourself.

　　② 唸出聲音來。***Read aloud***. 或 Read out loud.

　　③ 大聲唸出來。Read loudly.

【比較 2】

　　英文：Can you read aloud?

　　中文：你能唸出聲音來嗎？【正】

　　　　　你能夠大聲唸嗎？【誤】

　　　　　【「大聲唸」是 read loudly】

4

【比較3】 read 可接受詞，也可不接受詞。

中文： 看著書本唸出聲音來。

英文： Read the book aloud.【正】

Read aloud.【正】

【read 本身就有「看書」的意思，在此為不及物動詞】

Read it aloud.【正】

【it 不是指「課本」，而是指「課本內容」】

Read the text aloud.【正】

〔tɛkst〕*n.* 課文

Read the lesson aloud.【正】

【字面的意思是「唸出這一課。」】

下面的句子，都是美國老師在課堂上常說的話：

Read aloud. （唸出聲音來。）【最常用】

Read aloud, please. （請唸出聲音來。）【第二常用】

Read it aloud. （唸出聲音來。）【第三常用】

Read aloud, everybody.【第四常用】

（大家一起朗讀。）

Read aloud for me. （給我朗讀。）【第九常用】

Read aloud right now.【第七常用】

（立刻唸出聲音來。）

Read aloud together. （一起唸出來。）【第八常用】

I want you to read aloud.【第五常用】

（我要你們唸出聲音來。）

I'd like you to read aloud.【第六常用】

（我要你們唸出聲音來。）

4

Read aloud. 美國人也常說成 Read out loud.，兩者使用頻率相同。

【比較】 ***Read aloud***. (唸出聲音來；朗讀。)【正，常用】

Read out loud. 【正，常用】

(唸出聲音來；朗讀。)

Read out loudly. (大聲唸出來。)【正，常用】

Read it out loudly.

(把它大聲唸出來。)【正，常用】

Read loud. (大聲唸。)【正，極少用】

Read loudly. (大聲唸。)【正，常用】

2. *Read in unison*.

unison〔ˈjunəsn̩〕*n.* 和諧；一致；【音】齊唱

in unison ①和諧地 (= *in harmony*)

②同時 (= *at the same time*)

③一致地 (= *in agreement*)

④一起 (= *together*)

這句話的意思是「一起唸。」下面是按照使用頻率排列：

Read in unison. (一起唸。)【最常用】

= Read together. (一起唸。)【第二常用】

= Read it together. (一起唸。)【第三常用】

= Read it all together. (大家一起唸。)

= Read it at the same time. (同時唸。)

= Read it simultaneously. (同時唸。)

〔ˌsaɪml̩ˈtenɪəslɪ〕*adv.* 同時地

Read in unison. 也可說成：Read it in unison. 下面各句意義大致相同，都是老師在課堂上常說的話：

Read in unison.（一起唸。）【第一常用】

= Read it in unison.（一起唸。）【第二常用】

= Please read it in unison.（請一起唸。）【第三常用】

= I want everyone to read in unison.

（我要每個人都一起唸。）【第四常用】

= Read it in unison, class.【第五常用】

（各位同學一起唸。）

= Read it in unison, everybody.【第六常用】

（大家一起唸。）

3. *Read all together as one.*

all together 一起

as one 作「一致地」解，源自 as one person 或 as one voice。*as one* 的意思是「全體像一個人一樣」（ = *as if a group were one person* ）。

Read all together as one. 這句話的意思是「全體一起唸。」

【例】 They sang together *as one*.

（他們一起唱歌。）

We always work together *as one*.

（我們總是緊密地一起工作。）

The dancers moved *as one*.

（這些舞者的動作一致。）

4. *I'll say the first line.*

line〔laɪn〕*n.* 行

　　這句話的意思是「我將唸第一行。」這種說法和中國人的習慣不一樣,在「一口氣英語」中,每一行就是一句,像英文的詩或短文,只要第一行就是第一句時,美國人習慣用 line 來代替 sentence。

【比較1】　***I'll say the first line.***
　　　　　　【常用,第一行就是第一句時說】
　　　　　　I'll say the first sentence.
　　　　　　【常用,第一行就是第一句時,就較少說】

【比較2】　***I'll say the first line.***
　　　　　　【常用,美國人多用縮寫的 I'll 代替 I will】
　　　　　　I will say the first line.
　　　　　　【較少用,除非加強語氣】

I'll say the first line. 也可說成:

　　I'll say the first line by myself.
　　(我將自己唸第一行。)
　　I'll do the first line. (我將唸第一行。)
　　【在課堂上,老師常用 do 來代替 say, read 等。】
　　I'll say the first line alone.
　　　　　　　　　　　　〔ə'lon〕*adv.* 單獨地
　　(我將單獨唸第一行。)

如果老師看著書唸的時候,就說:

　　I'll read the first line. (我將唸第一行。)

5. *You repeat and continue.*

repeat〔rɪˈpit〕v. 重複；重說
continue〔kənˈtɪnju〕v. 繼續

這句話的意思是「你們跟著唸，繼續不要停。」

You repeat and continue.【最常用】
= Repeat and continue.【最常用】
= Repeat and continue on.【最常用】

= Repeat it and continue on.【較常用】
= Repeat after me and keep going.【較常用】
= Say it after me and keep on going.【較常用】

= Repeat it and continue reading.【常用】
= Say it after me and keep reading.【常用】
= Repeat it and continue speaking.【常用】
【repeat 後面可加 it，也可不加。】

在課堂上，叫同學繼續不要停，除了說 continue
以外，美國老師還常說：

Go on.（繼續。）
= Keep going.
= Keep doing it.

6. *Go on and on nonstop.*

on and on 繼續不斷地；一直不停地（= *without stopping*）

nonstop〔'nɑn'stɑp〕*adv.* 不斷地（= *continuously*）；

不停地（= *without stopping*）

nonstop 很多美國人會寫成 *non-stop*（誤），
但是，在所有大字典上，都寫成 nonstop。

Go *on and on* **nonstop**.

這句話短，一口氣唸完，不要停頓，意思是
「繼續不要停。」這句話也可以說成：You go on
and on nonstop.（你們繼續不要停。）也可以客
氣一點說：Please go on and on nonstop.（請
繼續不要停。）也可以加強語氣，說成：Keep
going on and on nonstop.（繼續不要停止。）

叫同學不停地唸，還可以說：

Read on and on nonstop.（繼續不停地唸。）
Speak on and on nonstop.（繼續不停地說。）
Say it on and on nonstop.（繼續不停地說。）

4

7. *Don't let up.*

let up ①放鬆；減弱；變小；減慢
②停止（= *come to a stop*）

let up 在各種不同的句中，有各種不同的解釋，主要的意思是「減慢」（= *slow down*）或「變小」（= *diminish*）、「放鬆」、「減弱」，甚至「停止」。

像 Don't *let up* until you finish your job. 這句話的意思，可能是 ① 在你做完工作以前，不要放鬆。② 在你做完工作以前，不要停止。所以 *let up* 這個成語的意思是從「放鬆」、「減弱」、「變小」，甚至到「停止」都有。

所有的字典都沒清楚說明 *let up* 這個成語，我們一定要徹底研究。

let up 起源自早期美國人駕馬車，當把繮繩往上拉（let up on the reins）的時候，馬就會「減慢」速度，如果拉得強烈一點，就會「停止」。所以，在進行中的動作，不是突然停止的，就可用 *let up*，來表示減慢或停止。在不同的句中，有不同的解釋，原則上，*let up* 介於減慢或停止中。

(1) He lost the race because he *let up* at the end.

（他跑輸了，因為他到最後，速度減慢了。）

【lose〔luz〕*v.* 輸掉　race〔res〕*n.* 賽跑
let up 減慢（= *slow down*）】

(2) Top students never ***let up***. They always try their

best. (好學生從來不放鬆。他們總是盡全力。)

【top〔tɑp〕*adj.* 頂尖的　***let up*** 放鬆 (= *take it easy*)】

(3) Traffic ***lets up*** after rush hour.

(尖峰時間過後，交通流量就減少了。)

【***let up*** 減少 (= *diminish*)　***rush hour*** (交通) 尖峰時間】

4

(4) She studies all day long without ***letting up*** once.

(她整天不停地唸書。)

【***let up*** 停止 (= *stop*)；休息 (= *take a break*)】

(5) The rain finally ***let up***.

(①雨終於停了。②雨終於變小了。)

【***let up*** ①停止 (= *stop*)；② (雨) 變小 (= *slow down*)】

(6) Pursue your goals. Don't ***let up*** till you

achieve them.

(追求你的目標。在達成之前都不要放鬆。)

【***let up*** ①停止 (= *stop*)；②放鬆 (= *take it easy*)】

(7) ***Let up*** a little. You're working too hard.

(休息一會吧。你太辛苦了。)

【***let up*** 放鬆 (= *take it easy*)】

(8) Don't ***let up***. Keep at it!

(①不要停止，繼續努力！ ②不要放鬆，繼續努力！)

【***let up*** ①停止 (= *stop*)；②放鬆 (= *take it easy*)】

(9) Shopping always ***lets up*** after the Christmas

season. (聖誕節假期過後，買東西的人就少了。)

【***let up*** 減慢 (= *slow down*)；減少 (= *diminish*)

season〔'sizn〕*n.* 時期】

8. *Keep at it!*

    keep at 繼續做

    Keep at it! 繼續做下去！；堅持下去！

        Keep at it! 已經是一個慣用句，美國老師常説：

        Keep at it! Don't stop no matter what.

        （堅持下去！無論如何都不要停止。）

        Keep at it until you finish it.

        （做完才停止。）

        Keep at it until you solve it.

        （繼續做到你解決它為止。）【solve〔sɑlv〕*v.* 解決】

    Keep at it!

= Keep working at it!

  【例】 Keep working at it! Don't stop till I
        say so. (繼續做下去！我說停才停。)
        【so 是代名詞，代替 stop。】

9. *Keep going no matter what.*

    keep + V-ing 繼續   go〔go〕*v.* 進行

        這句話的意思是「無論發生什麼事，都要繼
    續進行。」在這裡的意思就是「無論如何，都要
    繼續唸。」

【比較 1】

Keep going *no matter what.*【最常用】

（無論如何，都不要停。）

Keep on going *no matter what.*【較常用】

（無論如何，都要繼續進行，再接再勵。）

在「一口氣英語① p.44」已經提到 keep + V-ing
表「繼續做某事」中間不停，keep on + V-ing 表
「繼續做某事」，中間有停頓。

【比較 2】

Keep going no matter what.

Keep going on no matter what.【語氣較強】

（無論如何，都要繼續進行。）

這兩句話句意相同，go on 等於 continue，所以語氣較強。

【比較 3】

Keep going ***no matter what.***【最常用】

Keep going ***no matter what*** *happens.*【較常用】

（無論發生什麼事，都要繼續進行。）

Keep going no matter what may happen.

（無論會發生什麼事，都要繼續進行。）

【像是課本英文，口語中少用。】

　no matter what 可放在任何句尾，來加強語氣，
它是一個副詞子句的省略，源自 ***no matter what***
happens 或 ***no matter what*** *may happen*。

例如，美國人常說：

Never lie, cheat or steal, *no matter what*.

（無論如何，都不要說謊、欺騙，或偷竊。）

【這句話是美國西點軍校的座右銘】

【lie〔laɪ〕*v.* 說謊　　cheat〔tʃit〕*v.* 欺騙
steal〔stil〕*v.* 偷】

Listen to your parents *no matter what*.

（無論如何都要聽你父母的話。）

【美國父母在小孩十八歲以前，常會說這句話，就像
我們中國人說「要孝順父母」，一樣常用。】

Take care of your health *no matter what*.

（無論如何，都要照顧自己的健康。）

Stay in touch *no matter what*.

（無論如何，都要保持連絡。）

Don't quit *no matter what*.

（無論如何，都不要放棄。）

【quit〔kwɪt〕*v.* 停止；放棄】

Always try *no matter what*.

（無論如何，總是要試一試。）

【對話練習 1】

A： Read aloud.

B： Where should I start?
　　Where should I stop?
　　How fast or slow should
　　I go?

A： Read in unison.

B： Whatever you say.
　　We do it all the time.
　　Please tell us when to begin.

A： Read all together as one.

B： We're all set. 〔sɛt〕*adj.* 準備好的
　　We're ready to begin.
　　We're waiting for your signal.
　　【signal〔'sɪgn!〕*n.* 信號】

A： I'll say the first line.

B： I understand.
　　I'll listen carefully.
　　I'll let you go first.

A： 唸出聲音來。

B： 我該從哪裡開始？
　　我該在哪裡停止？
　　我該唸多快或多慢？

4

A： 一起唸。

B： 我們聽你的。
　　我們總是一起唸。
　　請告訴我們何時開始。

A： 全體一起唸。

B： 我們都準備好了。
　　我們準備好要開始唸了。
　　我們在等你的信號。

A： 我將唸第一行。

B： 我了解。
　　我會仔細聽。
　　我會讓你先唸。

【對話練習 2】

A：You repeat and continue.

B：I'll follow you.
　　I'll repeat after you.
　　I'll continue on and on.

A：Go on and on nonstop.

B：Yes, sir.
　　We'll keep going.
　　We won't stop till you say so.

A：Don't let up.

B：Don't worry.
　　I won't let up.
　　I'll give it one hundred
　　percent.
　　【*give it one hundred percent* 盡力】

A：Keep at it!

B：I'll keep at it.
　　I'll keep on going.
　　I promise I won't give up.
　　【*give up* 放棄】

A：你跟著唸，繼續不要停。

B：我會跟著你唸。
　　我會跟著你唸。
　　我會繼續不停地唸。

A：繼續不要停。

B：是的，老師。
　　我們會持續下去。
　　你說停，我們才會停。

A：不要停止。

B：別擔心。
　　我不會停止。
　　我會盡全力。

A：堅持下去！

B：我會堅持下去。
　　我會持續下去。
　　我保證不會放棄。

5. *Time to recite.*

Time to recite.
Time to remember.
Let's practice and rehearse.

No books allowed.
Rely on your memory.
Show me what you know.

Who volunteers?
Who's first?
You all must take a turn.

---

recite〔rɪ'saɪt〕
remember〔rɪ'mɛmbɚ〕
practice〔'præktɪs〕   rehearse〔rɪ'hɝs〕
allow〔ə'laʊ〕   *rely on*
memory〔'mɛmərɪ〕   show〔ʃo〕
volunteer〔ˌvɑlən'tɪr〕   *take a turn*

【內文解説】

Time to recite.	是該背書的時間了。
Time to remember.	是該記住的時候了。
Let's practice and rehearse.	我們練習練習吧。
No books allowed.	不准看書。
Rely on your memory.	要靠你們的記憶力。
Show me what you know.	告訴我你們知道些什麼。
Who volunteers?	有誰自願試一試？
Who's first?	哪一位先？
You all must take a turn.	你們全都要輪到。

** ───────────────────

recite 〔rɪ'saɪt〕 v. 朗讀；背誦
remember 〔rɪ'mɛmbɚ〕 v. 記住；記得
practice 〔'præktɪs〕 v. 練習
rehearse 〔rɪ'hɝs〕 v. 排練；演練
allow 〔ə'laʊ〕 v. 允許　　*rely on* 依靠；依賴
memory 〔'mɛmərɪ〕 n. 記憶力　　show 〔ʃo〕 v. 給…看
volunteer 〔,vɑlən'tɪr〕 v. 自願　　*take a turn* 輪流

【背景説明】

　　「一口氣英語」的教法是，老師講解後，帶同學唸，同學看著課本一起唸，唸熟以後，就開始全體一起來背了。大家都快要背熟的時候，再讓每位同學單獨試著背。

1. ***Time to recite.***
   recite〔rɪ'saɪt〕*v.* 朗讀；背誦

　　　　這句話的意思是「該是背書的時間了。」源自
　　It's time to recite.

　　　　這類的說法很多，下面是按照使用頻率排列：

① Time to recite. 【第一常用】
　（該是背書的時間了。）
② It's time to recite. 【第二常用】
　（該是背書的時間了。）
③ It's time for us to recite. 【第三常用】
　（該是我們背書的時間了。）

④ Let's recite. (我們來背書吧。)
⑤ Now, let's recite. (現在，我們來背書吧。)

⑥ Now, it's time to recite.
　（現在，該是背書的時間了。）
⑦ Now, it's time for us to recite.
　（現在，該是我們背書的時間了。）

5

⑧ It's time for recitation. (是該背書的時間了。)

〔͵rɛsə'teʃən 〕 *n.* 背誦；朗誦

⑨ It's time to practice recitation.

(是該練習背書的時間了。)

⑩ Let's do some recitation. (我們來背點書吧。)

⑪ Let's have some recitation.

(我們來背點書吧。)

2. ***Time to remember.***

remember 〔 rɪ'mɛmbɚ 〕 *v.* 記住；記得

這句話的意思是「該是記住的時候了。」源自

It's time to remember what we've learned.

(該是記住我們所學過的東西的時候了。)

【比較】 Time to remember. 【最常用，一般語氣】

It's time to remember. 【較常用，語氣稍強】

It's time for us to remember. 【常用，語氣最強】

(該是我們記住的時候了。)

3. ***Let's practice and rehearse.***

practice 〔'præktɪs 〕 *v.* 練習

rehearse 〔 rɪ'hɝs 〕 *v.* 預演；排練；練習；演練

在 Roget's College Thesaurus 字典中，
rehearse 的同義字有 repeat, recite, practice,
drill 等。英文裡面往往會用相同意思的動詞，
來加強語氣。

【比較】下面三句話，意思相同，語氣不同：

Let's practice. (我們練習吧。)【一般語氣】

Let's practice and rehearse. 【加強語氣】

(我們練習練習吧。)

Let's practice, rehearse and drill. 【語氣最強】

(我們不斷地練習吧。)　〔drɪl〕*v.* 反覆練習

下面三句話，和 ***Let's practice and rehearse.***
意思相同：

5

Let's go over it some more.

(我們再練習練習吧。)【*go over* 重讀；複習】

Let's do it over and over.

(我們不斷地練習吧。)

Let's do it again and again.

(我們不斷地練習吧。)

【*over and over* 再三地 (= *again and again*)】

有老師在問，Let's 和 Let us 有何不同？

Let's 是表「建議」，Let us 是表「請求」。

【比較】 Let's go, shall we? (我們走吧，好嗎？)

Let us go, will you? (讓我們走，可以嗎？)

關於附加問句的用法，詳見「文法寶典」p.7。

4. *No books allowed.*

allow〔ə'laʊ〕*v.* 允許

allow 通常當及物動詞用，這句話源自 No books are allowed.（正）意思是「不准看書。」（= *No looking at your books.*）

"No + 名詞" 和 "No + V-ing" 一樣，都表示「禁止～」。

"No + 名詞 + allowed." 有加強語氣的意味。

【比較1】 下面兩句話一樣常用，但語氣不同：

No books.（不能看書。）【一般語氣】

No books allowed.（不准看書。）【語氣稍強】

【比較2】

No books are allowed.【文法對，美國老師少用】

No books allowed.【省略 are，美國老師常說】

$$\text{"No} + \begin{Bmatrix} \text{名詞} \\ \text{動名詞} \end{Bmatrix} + \text{allowed."}$$ 雖然在文法上

很難解釋，但美國人常說，我們一定要學會。

【例】 No smoking allowed.

（不准抽煙。）

No talking allowed.

（不准交談。）【老師在課堂上說】

No food or drinks allowed.

（禁止飲食。）【在大眾運輸工具上常見】

No pets allowed.【在有些商店、建築物門口常見】
(禁止攜帶寵物。)【pet〔pɛt〕n. 寵物】
No minors allowed. (未成年者不得進入。)
〔'maɪnɚz〕n. pl. 未成年者
No cell phones allowed. (不得使用大哥大。)
【*cell phone* 大哥大；行動電話】

No books allowed. 也可以説成：

Don't look at your books. (不要看書本。)
Put your books away. (把你們的書本收起來。)
Close your books. (把你們的書本合起來。)
【*put away* 收拾】

5

5. *Rely on your memory.*

rely on 依靠；依賴　　memory〔'mɛmərɪ〕n. 記憶力

這句話的意思是「要靠你們的記憶力。」

【比較】 rely on 和 depend on 同義，但是在這
裡不能使用 depend on。

Rely on your memory.【正】
Depend on your memory.
【誤，depend on 通常是指「依靠」他人。】

這句話也可以説成：

Just rely on your memory.
(只要靠著你們的記憶力。)
Just rely on what you've learned.
(只要靠著你們所學的。)
Just rely on what you know.
(只要靠著你們所知道的。)

6. ***Show me what you know.***

show〔ʃo〕v. 給…看

這句話的字面意思是「給我看你們知道什麼。」
引申為「告訴我你們知道些什麼。」也可以說成：
Show me what you can do. (告訴我你們能做什
麼。) 或 Show me what you've learned. (告訴
我你們所學到的。)

【比較】 t 碰到 u 的時候，通常會連音。

Show me what you know.【極少用】
　　　　　〔hwɑt〕〔ju〕
Show me what you know.【常用】
　　　　　　〔'hwɑtʃu〕

7. ***Who volunteers?***

volunteer〔ˌvɑlən'tɪr〕v. 自願　n. 自願者

這句話的意思是「有誰自願試一試？」

這種說法很多，**volunteer** 當動詞的時候，
常說的有：

Who volunteers?【最常用】
Does anyone ***volunteer?***【較常用】
(有誰自願試一試？)
Does anyone want to ***volunteer?***【常用】
(有人想自願試一試？)

Who wants to *volunteer*?【最常用】

（誰想自願試一試？）

Who would like to *volunteer*?【較常用】

（誰想自願試一試？）

I want everyone to *volunteer*.【常用】

（我要大家自願試一試。）

volunteer 當名詞時，美國老師在課堂上常說的句子如下，我們按照使用頻率排列：

① Any *volunteers?*【第一常用】

（有人自願試一試嗎？）

② Are there any *volunteers*?【第二常用】

（有誰自願試一試？）

③ Do I have any *volunteers*?

（有誰自願試一試？）

④ I'd like some *volunteers*.

（我希望有人自願來試一試。）

⑤ I want some *volunteers*.

（我需要有人自願來試一試。）

⑥ Do we have any *volunteers*?

（有人自願要試一試嗎？）

8. *Who's first?*

這句話的意思是「哪一位先？」也可說成：
Who's going to be first? (誰要第一個上來？)
或 Who's going to take the first turn? (誰要輪第一個？)

【比較】 *Who's first?* (哪一位先？)
　　　　 Who goes first?

　　　　　①哪一位先？【事先未排好順序】
　　　　　②誰是第一個？【事先已排好順序】

當第一位同學上台以後，老師可以說：

Who's ready? (誰準備好了？)【最常用】
Who's ready to go?【第二常用】
　　　　　〔 go 〕v. 開始；開始進行
(誰準備好要上來試一試了？)
Who's willing to go?
　　　　　〔'wɪlɪŋ〕adj. 願意的
(誰願意上來試一試？)【第六常用】

Who's willing?【第五常用】
(有誰願意上來試一試？)
Who wants to go? (有誰想來試一試？)【第三常用】
Who'd like to go? (有誰想要試一試？)【第四常用】

9. *You all must take a turn.*

take a turn 輪流

這句話的意思是「你們全部都要輪到。」也有
美國老師說：

Everyone take a turn.
（每個人都要輪到。）
【本句是命令句，Everyone 是稱呼語，所以須用
原形動詞 take，而不能用 takes。】
Every student will take a turn.
（每個同學都會輪到。）
Every student must take a turn.
（每個同學都必須輪到。）

【比較】take a turn 和 take turns 都表示「輪流」，
但意義不同：

You all must *take a turn*.
（你們全部都要輪到。）
You all must *take turns*.
（你們全部都必須輪流。）

take a turn 是指「輪流一次」，*take turns*
是「互相輪流」，也許不只一次，例如叫小孩子
輪流玩玩具，或是輪流做某事，後面常加動名
詞，如：Please *take turns* reading the book.
（請輪流看這本書。）

在成語書中，我們常看到的 *by turns*，是由 *by taking turns* 省略而來。美國人日常生活中，較少用 by turns。

【比較】

You all must recite *by turns*. 【較少用】

（你們都必須輪流背。）

You all must recite *by taking turns*. 【較常用】

（你們都必須輪流背。）

5

in turn（依序地）和 *by turns*（輪流）意思不完全相同：

【例】 You all must recite *in turn*.

（你們都必須按次序地背誦。）

Please come up to the blackboard *in turn*.

（請一個接一個地到黑板前面來。）

blackboard〔'blæk͵bord 〕*n.* 黑板

in turn 是按照原先排定的次序，不輪第二次，而 *by turns* 可以輪到第二次或第二次以上。

【對話練習 1】

A：Time to recite.

B：OK, I'm ready.
　　I like to recite.
　　It's a great way to learn.

A：Time to remember.

B：Let's go for it.
　　Let's try to remember.
　　Remembering is the key.
　　【*go for it* 勇敢地試一試
　　key〔ki〕*n.* 關鍵】

A：Let's practice and rehearse.

B：That's fine with me.
　　I need lots of practice.
　　Practice makes perfect.
　　【perfect〔'pɝfɪkt〕*adj.* 完美的】

A：No books allowed.

B：I agree with it.
　　That's a good rule.
　　We all must learn to
　　remember.

A：是該背書的時間了。

B：好的，我準備好了。
　　我喜歡背書。
　　那是個學習的好方法。

A：是該記住的時候了。

B：我們勇敢地試一試吧。
　　我們努力記住吧。
　　記住是關鍵。

A：我們練習練習吧。

B：我沒問題。
　　我需要多練習。
　　熟能生巧。

A：不准看書。

B：我同意。
　　那是個好的規定。
　　我們都必須學習記住。

5

【對話練習 2】

A：Rely on your memory.

B：That's a challenge for me.
My memory is poor.
I get nervous and then I
forget.
【challenge (ˈtʃælɪndʒ) *n.* 挑戰
poor (pur) *adj.* 差的
nervous (ˈnɝvəs) *adj.* 緊張的】

A：Who volunteers?

B：I volunteer.
I'm willing to try.
You can pick me.
【pick (pɪk) *v.* 挑選】

A：Who's first?

B：I'll go first.
I'd like to go first.
I don't mind going first.

A：You all must take a turn.

B：That's fair.
That's the best way.
That's the smart way to do it.
【fair (fɛr) *adj.* 公平的
smart (smɑrt) *adj.* 聰明的】

A：要靠你們的記憶力。

B：那對我而言是項挑戰。
我的記性很差。
我會緊張，然後就會忘
記了。

A：有誰自願試一試？

B：我自願。
我願意試一試。
你可以選我。

A：哪一位先？

B：我先出來試一試。
我想要先試一試。
我不介意先試一試。

A：你們全部都要輪到。

B：那很公平。
那是最好的方式。
那樣做很聰明。

6. *Go for it!*

Go for *it!*
Just do *it!*
Give *it* a try.

Give it a shot.
You can do it.
You have nothing to lose.

Get up here.
Get out of your seat.
Come on up and try.

---

try〔traɪ〕
lose〔luz〕
seat〔sit〕

shot〔ʃɑt〕
get out of

【內文解說】

Go for *it!*	勇敢地試一試！
Just do *it!*	趕快做！
Give *it* a try.	試一試。
Give it a shot.	試一試。
You can do it.	你們能夠做得到。
You have nothing to lose.	你們沒什麼損失。
Get up here.	到前面來。
Get out of your seat.	站起來。
Come on up and try.	趕快到前面來試一試。

6

** ————————————————

go for it 勇敢地試一試　　*just do it* 趕快做
try〔traɪ〕*n.* 嘗試　　*give it a try* 試一試
shot〔ʃɑt〕*n.* 射擊；嘗試　　*give it a shot* 試一試
lose〔luz〕*v.* 損失　　*get out of* 離開
seat〔sit〕*n.* 座位

【背景說明】

當上一回説完 Who volunteers? Who's first? You all must take a turn. 之後，如果還是沒有同學要上台，老師就可以接著講下面這九句話。

1. *Go for it!*

這句話字面的意思是「要為它而努力！」引申為「試一試！」或「勇敢地試一試！」相當於 Try it! 或 Do it!。

【例】 What are you waiting for? *Go for it!*
（你還在等什麼？要大膽試一試啊！）
Don't wait! *Go for it!*
（不要等了！試一試！）

【比較】 *Go for it!*（勇敢地試一試！）【語氣較強】
Try it.（試一試。）【語氣較弱】
【注意 Try it. 無驚嘆號】

這兩句話意義不同。當別人不想嘗試，你鼓勵他勇敢地試一試時，你就説：Go for it! 如果你拿了一杯飲料，叫別人試一試，你就可以説：Try it. Drink some.
（試一試。喝一些。）

2. *Just do it!*

　　Just do it! 是美國人的口頭禪，美國的 Nike〔'naɪki〕公司，就用這句話做標語，字面的意思是「只要做它！」引申為「趕快做！」因為美國人一般只喜歡說，不喜歡做，Nike 用這個標語的目的，在於鼓勵人們付諸行動。

【比較】 *Just do it!*（趕快做！）【語氣較強】
　　　　Do it!（趕快做！）【語氣強】

美國老師在課堂上常說：

　　Do it!（趕快做！）【最常用】
　　Do it now!（現在就做！）【最常用】

　　Just do it!（趕快做！）【最常用】
　　Just do it now!（現在就做！）【較常用】
　　Just do it right now!（立刻就做！）【較常用】

　　Please just do it!（請趕快做！）【常用】
　　Just do it, please!（請趕快做！）【較常用】

　　I want you to do it.【常用】
　　（我要你們趕快做。）
　　I want you to do it right now.【常用】
　　（我要你們立刻做。）
　　I'm asking you to do it.（我要你們去做。）【常用】

　　Just do it! 要翻成「趕快做！」或「採取行動吧！」、「做就對了！」，要看前後句意來決定。

【例】 What are you waiting for? ***Just do it!***

（你還在等什麼？趕快做！）

Stop talking about it. ***Just do it!***

（不要再談這件事了。採取行動吧！）

【Just do it! 在此等於 Just take action!】

Say no more. ***Just do it!***

（不要再說了。去做就對了！）

3. ***Give it a try.***

try〔traɪ〕 *n.* 嘗試

這句話的意思是「試一試。」等於 Try. 或 Try it. 下面是有關 try 的說法，我們按照使用頻率排列：

① ***Give it a try.***（試一試。）【第一常用】

② You must give it a try.【第二常用】

（你們必須試一試。）

③ You should give it a try.【第三常用】

（你們應該試一試。）

④ I want you to give it a try.

（我要你們試一試。）

⑤ I'd like you to give it a try.

（我希望你們能試一試。）

⑥ Everyone has to give it a try.

（大家都必須試一試。）

【比較】 ***Give it a try.***（試一試。）【較嚴肅】

Give it a shot.（試一試。）

【較幽默，男人比較喜歡說】

4. *Give it a shot.*

shot〔ʃɑt〕*n.* 射擊；嘗試

shot 的主要意思是「射擊」，用槍射擊，不見得能射中，所以引申為「嘗試」(= *a try at sth.*)。*Give it a shot.* 的意思就是「試一試。」等於 Give it a try.

下面是美國老師在課堂上常說的話，我們按照使用頻率排列：

① *Give it a shot.*（試一試。）【第一常用】
② You must give it a shot.【第二常用】
   （你們必須試一試。）
③ You have to give it a shot.【第三常用】
   （你們必須試一試。）

④ I want you to give it a shot.
   （我要你們試一試。）
⑤ Come on, give it a shot.
   （好啦，試一試。）
⑥ I want everyone to give it a shot.
   （我要大家都試一試。）

5. *You can do it.*

這句話字面的意思是「你們能夠做它。」引申為「你們能夠做得到。」美國人喜歡說鼓勵他人的話，這類同義的句子很多，我們按照使用的頻率排列：

You can do it.（你們能夠做得到。）【第一常用】
= You have the ability.（你們有能力。）【第二常用】
= You have what it takes.（你們很有能力。）
【這句話的用法，詳見「劉毅演講式英語①」p.9-12】

= You're up to it.（你們能勝任。）
= You're up to the task.（你們能勝任這個工作。）
= You're able to do it.（你們能夠做得到。）

【*be up to* 能勝任；能做　　task〔tæsk〕*n.* 任務；工作】

美國老師在課堂上，常常鼓勵同學說：

You can do it.（你們能夠做得到。）【最常用】
You really can do it.【最常用】
（你們真的能夠做得到。）
You can do anything.【較常用】
（你們任何事都做得到。）

You can do it if you try.【較常用】
（如果你們肯嘗試，就能做到。）
I know you can do it if you try.【較常用】
（我知道如果你們肯嘗試，就能做到。）
You can do anything if you try hard enough.
（如果你們夠努力，就能做到任何事。）【常用】

You can do it easily.【最常用】

（你們能輕易地做到。）

You can do it, no problem.【常用】

（你們能夠做到，沒問題的。）

You can do it, no problem at all.【常用】

（你們能夠做到，一點問題也沒有。）

6. ***You have nothing to lose.***

lose〔luz〕*v.* 損失

　　這句話的意思是「你們沒什麼損失。」也可以說成：You can't lose a thing.（你們一點都不會損失。）美國人常說：You have everything to gain. ***You have nothing to lose.***（你們什麼都能得到。你們什麼都不會損失。）

7. ***Get up here.***

　　在字典上，get up 是「起立；起床」的意思，但在這裡，up 是指「向前；靠近」。

　　叫別人「到前面來」時，就說 ***Get up here.***或 Come up here.；叫別人「進來」時，說 Get in here.；叫別人「到後面來」時，說 Get back here.當沒有前後之分的時候，可用 Come here.（來這裡。）或 Come over here.（過來這裡。）

所以，***Get up here.*** 中的 Get up，完全沒有「起立；起床」的意思。老師在課堂上，叫同學「到前面來」，不管同學原來是站著或坐著，都可說 ***Get up here.***

【比較】 中文： 到前面來。

英文： ***Get up here.*** 【最常用】

Come up here. 【第二常用】

Come to the front. 【第三常用】
〔frʌnt〕*n.* 前面

6

Get up here. 字典上找不到這句話，但美國老師在課堂上常說。下面都是美國老師常說的話，我們按照使用頻率排列：

① ***Get up here.*** （到前面來。）【第一常用】
② Get up here, please. 【第二常用】
（請到前面來。）
③ Come on, get up here. 【第三常用】
（好啦，到前面來。）

④ Get up here right now.
（立刻到前面來。）【*right now* 現在；立刻】
⑤ Get up here in front of the class.
（到全班同學前面來。）【*in front of* 在～面前】
⑥ Please get up here with me.
（請到前面我這裡來。）

⑦ I want you to get up here.

（我要你們到前面來。）

⑧ I want you to get up here with me.

（我要你們到前面我這裡來。）

⑨ I'd like you to come up here and recite.

（我要你們到前面來背書。）　　〔rɪ'saɪt〕*v.* 背誦

　　除了在課堂上以外，在日常生活中，也常用 *Get up here.* 例如，在公車上，你叫你的朋友到前面和你一起坐，你就可以說：Come on, *get up here* with me. （好啦，到前面來和我一起坐。）走在路上，叫你的朋友和你一起走，你就可以說：*Get up here.* Walk with me. （到前面來，和我一起走。）

6

8. *Get out of your seat.*

get out of 離開　　seat〔sit〕*n.* 座位

　　這句話字面的意思是「離開你的座位。」也就是「站起來。」（= *Stand up.*)，並未表示離開座位到其他地方去。

　　這類的說法有：

Get out of your seat. （站起來。）【第一常用】

Get out of your seat right now. 【第四常用】

（現在立刻站起來。）

Please get out of your seat. 【第二常用】

（請站起來。）

6

I want you to get out of your seat. 【第三常用】

（我要你站起來。）

You must get out of your seat. 【第五常用】

（你必須站起來。）

Get out of your seat and try it. 【第六常用】

（你站起來試試看。）

9. *Come on up and try.*

come on up 是 come on 和 come up 的結合，come on 是「趕快」(= *hurry up*)，come up 是「走上前來」。

凡是叫別人「到前面來」，就可以說 Come up. 叫別人「進來」，說 Come in. 叫別人「過來」，就是 Come over. 這些話都可以加上 on，變成：*Come on up*. (趕快到前面來。) *Come on in*. (趕快進來。) *Come on over*. (趕快過來。)

【比較】 Come up. (到前面來。)【一般語氣】

　　　　Come on up. (趕快到前面來。)【加強語氣】

Come on up and try. 的意思是「趕快到前面來試一試。」如果說 Come up and try. 就是「到前面來試一試。」

下面的話，你都可以在課堂上說：

I want you to come on up and try.
（我要你們趕快到前面來試一試。）
Please come here and try.
（請來這裡試一試。）
Come up here in front of the class and try.
（到全班同學前面來試一試。）

Come up here and give it a try.
（到前面來試一試。）
Come on up and give it a try.
（趕快到前面來試一試。）
Come on up here and try.
（趕快到前面這裡來試試看。）

【對話練習 1】

A : Go for it!

B : Give me some time.
   I'm going to try.
   I need to get ready first.

A : Just do it!

B : That's great advice.
   Those are wonderful words.
   I love to hear people say that.
   【advice〔əd'vaɪs〕*n.* 勸告；建議】

A : Give it a try.

B : Please be patient.
   I plan to try.
   I need a little more time.
   【patient〔'peʃənt〕*adj.* 有耐心的】

A : Give it a shot.

B : I'd love to try.
   I'm ready anytime.
   I'm ready right now.

A：勇敢地試一試！

B：給我一點時間。
   我會試一試。
   我必須先準備好。

A：趕快做！

B：那是個很棒的建議。
   那是很好的話。
   我喜歡聽別人這麼說。

A：試一試。

B：請要有耐心。
   我打算試一試。
   我還需要一點時間。

A：試一試。

B：我很想試一試。
   我隨時都準備好了。
   我現在準備好了。

6

【對話練習 2】

A：You can do it.

B：I know I can.
　　I know I can do it.
　　Thanks for encouraging me.
　　【encourage〔ɪnˈkɝɪdʒ〕v. 鼓勵】

A：Get up here.

B：As you wish.
　　I'm coming right now.
　　I'm on my way.
　　【*on one's way* 在途中】

A：Get out of your seat.

B：OK, I'm up.
　　I'm standing up.
　　What should I do now?

A：Come on up and try.

B：Here I come.
　　I'm not afraid.
　　I'll give it a try.

A：你能夠做得到。

B：我知道我能。
　　我知道我能夠做得到。
　　謝謝你鼓勵我。

A：到前面來。

B：我聽你的。
　　我立刻就來。
　　我就過來了。

A：站起來。

B：好的，我站起來了。
　　我現在站起來了。
　　現在我該做什麼？

A：趕快到前面來試一試。

B：我來了。
　　我不怕。
　　我會試一試。

6

7. *Take a break.*

Take a break.
Take a rest.
Everybody take five.

Go get some air.
Go get a drink.
Stand up and stretch.

Don't be late.
Don't make me wait.
Please be back on time.

7

---

break〔brek〕   *take a break*
rest〔rɛst〕   *take a rest*
take five   air〔ɛr〕
drink〔drɪŋk〕   stretch〔strɛtʃ〕
late〔let〕   *on time*

【內文解說】

Take a break.	休息一下。
Take a rest.	休息一下。
Everybody take five.	大家休息一下。
Go get some air.	去呼吸一點新鮮空氣。
Go get a drink.	去喝杯飲料。
Stand up and stretch.	站起來讓身體活動活動。
Don't be late.	不要遲到。
Don't make me wait.	不要讓我等。
Please be back on time.	請準時回來。

** ————————————————

break〔brek〕*n.* 休息時間　　***take a break*** 休息一下
rest〔rɛst〕*n.* 休息　　***take a rest*** 休息一下
take five 休息一下；休息五分鐘
air〔ɛr〕*n.* 空氣　　drink〔drɪŋk〕*n.* 飲料
stretch〔strɛtʃ〕*v.* 伸懶腰；舒展肢體
late〔let〕*adj.* 遲到的　　***on time*** 準時地

【背景說明】

老師上完一節課後，要下課休息一下的時候，就可以說這九句話。

1. ***Take a break.***
break〔brek〕*n.* 裂縫；休息時間
take a break 休息一下

break 的主要意思是「打破」，是動詞，break 當名詞時，主要意思是「裂縫」，在工作、上課時，作「休息時間」解。

下面是美國老師在課堂上常說的話，我們按照使用頻率排列：

① Take a break.（休息一下。）【第一常用】
② ***Let's take a break.***【第二常用】
  （我們休息一下吧。）
③ Time for a break.【第三常用】
  （休息時間到了。）

④ Take a break, everybody.
  （大家休息一下。）
⑤ Everyone take a break.（大家休息一下。）
  【Everyone 非主詞，是名詞當稱呼用】
⑥ It's time to take a break.
  （休息時間到了。）

7

⑦ Let's all take a break. (我們大家休息一下吧。)

⑧ You can take a break. (你們可以休息一下。)

⑨ We need to take a break. (我們需要休息一下。)

Time for a break. 也可説成 It's time for a break.
使用頻率相同。everybody 和 everyone 可以互換。

2. ***Take a rest.***

rest 〔 rɛst 〕 *n.* 休息

take a rest 休息一下 (= *take a break*)

這句話的意思是「休息一下。」

下面是美國老師在課堂上常説的話,我們按
照使用頻率排列:

① ***Take a rest.*** (休息一下。)

② Let's take a rest. (我們休息一下吧。)

③ Let's rest a while. (我們休息一會。)
　　　〔 rɛst 〕*v.* 休息

④ Let's all take a rest. (我們大家休息一下。)

⑤ Time for a rest. (休息時間到了。)

⑥ Time to take a rest. (休息時間到了。)

⑦ Everybody take a rest. (大家休息一下。)

⑧ Take a rest, everybody. (大家休息一下。)

⑨ It's time for a rest. (休息時間到了。)

⑩ It's time to take a rest. (休息時間到了。)

⑪ You can take a rest. (你們可以休息一下。)

⑫ We need to take a rest. (我們需要休息一下。)

3. *Everybody take five.*

take five 休息一下；休息五分鐘

take five 源自 take a five-minute break
（休息五分鐘），這句話由於已經講太多了，變成
慣用語，不一定是「休息五分鐘」，也可表示「休
息一下」(= *take a short break*)，通常指五到十
分鐘。如果是「休息十分鐘」，就要說 take a
ten-minute break，或 take ten。此時，並不像
take five 一樣，有「休息一下」的意味，而是指
「休息十分鐘」。

Everybody take five. 句中的 Everybody
並不是主詞，只是稱呼（詳見文法寶典 p.99），由於
句子短，everybody 後面不用加逗點，也可說成：
Take five, everybody. 這句話的意思是「大家休
息一下；大家休息五分鐘。」

美國老師在課堂上也常說：*Take five*, you
guys.（你們休息一下；你們休息五分鐘。）或
Go ahead and *take five*.（去休息一下吧；去休
息五分鐘吧。）

如果特別指定「休息五分鐘」，就說 Take
five minutes. 或 Take a five-minute break.

4. ***Go get some air.***

air〔ɛr〕*n.* 空氣

　　這句話字面的意思是「去得到一些空氣。」引申為「去呼吸一點新鮮空氣。」現在，美國人在 go 和 get 之間，一般都不加 to。

【比較1】 ***Go get some air.***
　　　　　【正，在短句中，go 後面的 and 或 to 要省略】
　　　　　Go to get some air.【正】
　　　　　（去呼吸一點新鮮空氣。）
　　　　　Go and get some air.
　　　　　【劣，文法對，但美國人不用】
　　　　　Go outside and get some air.【正】
　　　　　（去外面呼吸一點新鮮空氣。）

【比較2】 Get some air.【一般語氣】
　　　　　Go get some air.【語氣較強】
　　　　　Go get some fresh air.【語氣最強】
　　　　　　　　　　〔frɛʃ〕*adj.* 新鮮的

美國人非常喜歡用 ***go get***…。

【例】 Please ***go get*** some chalk for me.
　　　　　　　　　　　〔tʃɔk〕*n.* 粉筆
　　　（請你去拿一些粉筆給我。）

　　　Please ***go get*** the mail.（請你去把信拿過來。）
　　　　　　　　　　〔mel〕*n.* 信件

　　　Go get a good movie for tonight.
　　　（去弄一部好電影今晚來看看。）
　　　【movie 在此是指 DVD 或錄影帶。】

吃飯的時候，他們也常說 *Go get* 之類的句子，如：

Go get some spoons for dessert.

（去拿一些湯匙來吃甜點。）

【spoons〔spunz〕*n. pl.* 湯匙　dessert〔dɪˈzɜt〕*n.* 甜點】

Go get some more tea for our guests.

（再拿一些茶給我們的客人。）　〔gɛsts〕*n. pl.* 客人

Go get some napkins for us.

〔ˈnæpkɪnz〕*n. pl.* 餐巾紙

（去拿一些餐巾紙給我們。）

【napkins 在此指 paper napkins】

美國父母常叫小孩：

Go get a job.（去找份工作吧。）

Go get a haircut.（去理髮。）

〔ˈhɛrˌkʌt〕*n.* 理髮

Go get some gas for the car.（去給車子加點油。）

〔gæs〕*n.* 汽油

【這句話美國人常只說 Go get some gas.】

5. *Go get a drink.*

drink〔drɪŋk〕*n.* 飲料

這句話的意思是「去喝杯飲料。」也可以說成：

Get a drink.（去喝杯飲料。）或 You can go get
a drink.（你們可以去喝杯飲料。）

如果叫學生去喝水，就可以說：

Get some water.（去喝些水。）

Go get some water.（去喝些水。）

You can go get some water.（你們可以去喝些水。）

6. **_Stand up and stretch._**

stretch〔strɛtʃ〕*v.* 伸懶腰；舒展肢體

　　(= *extend one's muscles or limbs*)

　　　　這句話的意思是「站起來,讓身體活動活動。」
stretch 這個字,一般人不太會用,是及物和不及
物兩用動詞。

【例】 Always *stretch* before you exercise.

　　　　(運動前,一定要做熱身運動、舒展肢體。)

　　　 After sitting for a long time, you should
　　　 stand up and *stretch*.

　　　　(坐很久以後,你應該站起來,舒展肢體。)

　　　 Stretch your arms and legs every day.
　　　 It's very healthy. (每天伸伸手腳,有益健康。)

　　　 因爲伸展手的時候,都是伸「手臂」,所以美國人
　　　 都用 arms 來代替 hands,不可説成 *Stretch*
　　　 your hands and legs every day. (誤)】

7. **_Don't be late._**

late〔let〕*adj.* 遲到的

　　　　這句話的意思是「不要遲到。」也有美國老師
說:Please don't be late. (請不要遲到。) 或加強
語氣説成:Don't ever be late. (絕對不要遲到。)
或 Don't ever be late for class. (上課絕對不要遲
到。)【 *not ever* = never 表示「絕不」】

【比較】 **_Don't be late._** (不要遲到。)【 較常用 】

　　　　 Don't be late for class. 【 常用 】

　　　　　 (上課不要遲到。)

8. *Don't make me wait.*

這句話的意思是「不要讓我等。」美國老師也
常說：

Don't make me wait for you.

（不要讓我等你們。）

I hope you don't make me wait.

（我希望你們不要讓我等。）

Don't keep me waiting.（不要讓我等。）

make 是使役動詞，後要用原形動詞；keep
後面通常接現在分詞做受詞補語。Don't
keep me waiting. 和 Don't make me
wait. 一樣常用。

7

9. *Please be back on time.*

on time 準時地

這句話也可以說成：Please come back on
time. 或 Please get back on time. 意思都是「請
準時回來。」也有美國老師說：Don't get back
late.（回來不要遲到。）

【比較】 Please be back on time.【最常用】

Please be back in the classroom
on time.（請準時回到教室。）【較常用】

Please be back in class on time.【常用】

（請準時回來上課。）

10. 補充說明

Don't be late.
/e/

Don't make me wait.
/e/

Please be back on time.

　　這三句話很好背，因爲前面兩句開頭都是 *Don't*，
而且 late 和 wait 主要的母音都讀成 /e/，有押韻。
這三句話可以用在很多場合。

　　爲什麼背了「一口氣英語」，英文會説得比美國
人好呢？因爲美國人每天説的英文，他們自己也不
知道講得正確還是不正確，而我們所説的「一口氣
英語」，每句話都經過研究、每句話都精彩、每句話
都背到滾瓜爛熟，我們説起來當然有信心。

　　美國人説的話，寫出來往往錯誤百出，而我們
所説的英文，都可以正確地寫出來，所以，只要背了
「一口氣英語」，我們不管説和寫，都勝過美國人。

【對話練習 1】

A：Take a break.

B：I will if you will.
   That would be great.
   I really like that idea.
   【great〔gret〕*adj.* 很棒的】

A：Everybody take five.

B：Finally!
   Thank God!
   I've been waiting for so long.

A：Go get some air.

B：Let's go together.
   We need some fresh air.
   The air in here is bad.

A：Go get a drink.

B：Join me.
   Come with me.
   Let's quench our thirst.
   【join〔dʒɔɪn〕*v.* 加入
   quench〔kwɛntʃ〕*v.* 解（渴）
   thirst〔θɝst〕*n.* 口渴】

A：休息一下。

B：如果你願意，我會的。
   那真是太棒了。
   我真的很喜歡那個主意。

A：大家休息一下。

B：終於！
   謝天謝地！
   我等很久了。

A：去呼吸一點新鮮空氣。

B：我們一起去吧。
   我們需要一些新鮮空氣。
   這裡的空氣不好。

A：去喝杯飲料。

B：和我一起去吧。
   和我一起去吧。
   我們解解渴吧。

7

【對話練習 2】

A：Stand up and stretch.	A：站起來讓身體活動活動。
B：That's an excellent idea.	B：那是個很棒的主意。
It's a healthy thing to do.	這樣做有益健康。
Never sit for too long.	絕不要坐太久。
【healthy (ˈhɛlθɪ) adj. 健康的】	

A：Don't be late.	A：不要遲到。
B：Don't worry, I won't.	B：別擔心，我不會的。
I hate to be late.	我討厭遲到。
Being late is rude.	遲到不禮貌。
〔rud〕 adj. 無禮的	

7

A：Don't make me wait.	A：不要讓我等。
B：I promise, I won't.	B：我保證不會。
I'll be on time.	我會準時。
I won't make you wait.	我不會讓你等。

A：Please be back on time.	A：請準時回來。
B：I'll be here.	B：我會回來。
You have my word.	我向你保證。
I'll be back on time.	我會準時回來。
【one's *word* 諾言；保證】	

8. *Let's continue.*

Let's continue.
Let's carry on.
Let's get back to work.

Look alive!
*S*nap to it!
*S*how some life.

Heads *up*.
Sit *up* straight.
Get those shoulders back.

8

---

continue〔kən'tɪnjʊ〕	*carry on*
get back	alive〔ə'laɪv〕
Look alive!	snap〔snæp〕
Snap to it!	show〔ʃo〕
life〔laɪf〕	*sit up*
straight〔stret〕	shoulders〔'ʃoldəz〕

【內文解說】

Let's continue.	我們繼續吧。
Let's carry on.	我們繼續吧。
Let's get back to work.	我們繼續上課吧。
Look alive!	要振作起來！
*S*nap to it!	趕快！
*S*how some life.	要有精神。
Heads *up*.	頭抬起來。
Sit *up* straight.	坐直。
Get those shoulders back.	挺胸。

8

** ——————————————

continue〔kən'tɪnju〕v. 繼續　　***carry on*** 繼續
get back 回來　　alive〔ə'laɪv〕adj. 活著的；活潑的
Look alive! 振作起來！　　snap〔snæp〕v. 發出霹啪聲
Snap to it! 趕快！　　show〔ʃo〕v. 表現；顯露
life〔laɪf〕n. 生命；活力　　***sit up*** 坐起來；坐直
straight〔stret〕adv. 筆直地；挺直地
shoulders〔'ʃoldɚz〕n. pl. 肩膀

【背景説明】

　　如果同樣一位老師上兩堂課，第二節一上課，
老師就可以説這九句英語，作爲開場白。

1. *Let's continue.*

continue〔kən'tɪnjʊ〕*v.* 繼續

　　這句話的意思是「我們繼續吧。」等於 Let's
go on. 美國老師常説的話有：

Let's continue.（我們繼續吧。）【最常用】

Let's all continue.（我們大家繼續吧。）【第五常用】

Let's continue, please.（我們繼續吧，好嗎？）
【please 在此作「好嗎」、「行嗎」解。】【第七常用】

Let's continue on.（我們繼續吧。）【第二常用】

Let's continue studying.【第三常用】
（我們繼續學習吧。）

Let's continue studying the lesson.【第八常用】
（我們繼續學習這一課吧。）

Let's continue working on this lesson.【第九常用】
（我們繼續上這一課吧。）【*work on* 從事於；致力於】

Let's continue with today's lesson.【常用】
（我們繼續上今天的課吧。）

Let's all continue studying this lesson.【第六常用】
（我們大家繼續上這一課吧。）

8

Let's continue with class. 【第四常用】
（我們繼續上課吧。）
Let's continue on with this lesson. 【常用】
（我們繼續上這一課吧。）
Let's continue practicing this material. 【常用】
（我們繼續練習這個教材吧。）
【material〔mə'tɪrɪəl〕 *n.* 資料；教材】

2. *Let's carry on.*
   carry on 繼續 (= *continue*)

這句話的意思是「我們繼續吧。」(= *Let's continue.*) 如果是「繼續做某事」，就說成 *carry on with*～。

下面是美國老師常說的話：

Let's *carry on* with this lesson. 【最常用】
（我們繼續上這一課吧。）
Let's *carry on* and get going. 【較常用】
（我們繼續，開始吧。）
Let's *carry on*, starting from where we left off. （我們繼續吧，從我們上次結束的地方開始。）
【常用，*leave off* 停止】

Let's *carry on* with what we were doing.
（我們繼續上課吧。）【較常用】
Let's *carry on* and finish this lesson. 【常用】
（我們繼續把這一課上完吧。）
Let's *carry on* with Lesson Four.
（我們繼續上第四課吧。）【最常用】

3. *Let's get back to work.*

   get back 回來（ = *return* ）

      很奇怪，字典上不容易找到 get back 這個成語，但美國人常說。如你看到朋友要出遠門，你就可以說：You're leaving. When will you get back?（你要走了。你什麼時候回來？）看到朋友回來了，你就可以問：When did you get back?（你什麼時候回來的？）

      老師在課堂上說 *Let's get back to work.* 這句話的意思就是「我們繼續上課吧。」也可以說成：Let's go back to work. 或 Let's return to work. 這裡的 work 是指「學習」，是動詞。

【比較】 *Let's get back to work.*【work 是動詞】
         （我們繼續上課吧。）
      Let's get back to the work we were doing.
         （我們繼續上我們上的課吧。）【work 是名詞】

8

美國老師上課也常說：
   Let's all get back to our work right now.
   （我們大家現在繼續上課吧。）
   I want you to get back to work.
   （我希望你們繼續上課。）
   【want 可以作「要；想要；希望」解。】
   I'd like everyone to get back to work.
   （我要大家繼續上課。）

4. *Look alive!*

alive〔ə'laɪv〕*adj.* 活著的；活潑的

　　這句話字面的意思是「要看起來是活的！」美國人常說 *Look alive!* 這句話已經成為慣用句，有三個主要的意思：①振作起來；要有精神！②趕快！③加油！

【例1】 *Look alive!* Show some spirit! Look like you're ready to learn.〔'spɪrɪt〕*n.* 精神

（要振作起來！要有精神啊！你們要看起來準備好要上課了。）

【這些話是美國老師上課時常說的話，這裡的 Look alive! 等於 Be alert!〔ə'lɜt〕*adj.* 警覺的；注意的】

【例2】 *Look alive!* You'll be late.

（趕快！你要遲到了。）【*Look alive! = Hurry!*】

【例3】 Time for class. *Look alive*, everybody.

（上課的時間到了。大家要振作起來。）

【*look alive = be alert*】

【例4】 What's wrong? *Look alive!*

（怎麼了？要振作起來！）

【當你看到一個人無精打采的時候，就可說這句話。*Look alive! = Be alert!*】

【例5】 The coach yelled, "*Look alive*, everybody!"

（教練喊道：「大家加油！」）

【coach〔kotʃ〕*n.* 教練　　yell〔jɛl〕*v.* 喊叫

look alive = play harder】

【例6】 When you go for a job interview, always *look alive*.（當你去面試時，一定要有精神。）

【interview〔'ɪntɚˏvju〕*n.* 面試】

從上面的例句可以知道，***Look alive!*** 最主要的意思就是「要有精神；振作起來！」它的相反的意思是 ***look dead*** 「沒有精神；無精打采」。如，***You look dead.*** Did you sleep last night? (你看起來沒有精神。你昨天晚上有沒有睡覺？)

當你進到教室，看到同學死氣沈沈，你就可以說：

You guys look dead. ***Look alive!***

(你們這些人看起來死氣沈沈。要打起精神！)

【此時的 Look alive! 等於 Be alert! 】

5. ***Snap to it!***

snap〔snæp〕v. 發出霹啪聲

中指和大拇指用力摩擦出聲，就叫作 snap。***Snap to it!*** 源自當叫別人快一點的時候，會用兩個手指摩擦出聲音，所以，***Snap to it!*** 意思就是「趕快！」(= *Hurry!* = *Hurry up!*)

8

【例1】 We're late. ***Snap to it!***
(我們遲到了。快點！)

【例2】 ***Snap to it!*** We've got lots to do.
(快一點！我們有很多事要做。)

【例3】 You can do more than that. ***Snap to it!***
(你可以做得更多。快一點！)
【這句話通常是老闆對員工說。】

6. ***Show some life.***

show〔 ʃo 〕*v.* 表現;顯露
life〔 laɪf 〕*n.* 生命;活力

這句話字面的意思是「表現一些生命。」源自 *Show me some signs of life.* (給我看一些生命的跡象。) 引申爲「要有精神。」和 Look alive! 句意相同。任何時候,你看到同學沒有精神,你都可以說: Look alive! ***Show some life.*** (要振作起來啊!要有精神。)

Show some life. 也可以說成 Show me some life.

【比較1】 Show some life. 【正,常用】
Show me some life. 【正,較少用】
Show some life to me. 【正,較少用】

【比較2】 ***Show some life.*** 【最常用】
= ***Show some spirit.*** 【最常用】
= Show some energy. 【常用】
〔ˈɛnədʒɪ 〕*n.* 精力;活力
【前面兩句使用頻率相同】

7. *Heads up.*

這句話的意思是「頭抬起來。」源自 Get your heads up. (把你們的頭抬起來。)

【比較】

中文： 把頭抬起來。

英文： Raise your heads. 【正，常用】
Heads up. 【正，最常用】
Get your heads up. 【正，較常用】
Pick your heads up. 【正，較常用】
Lift your heads up. 【正，常用】

Get up your heads. 【誤】
Pick up your heads. 【正，常用】
Lift up your heads. 【正，常用】
【*get~up* 把~抬高　*pick up* 抬高 (= *lift up*)】

8

老師在課堂上，可以跟同學説：

Heads up. Look at me.
(頭抬起來，看著我。)
Get your heads up, and look up here.
(把你們的頭抬起來，看這裡。)
Heads up, everybody. Pay attention to me.
(大家頭抬起來。注意聽我說。)

8. ***Sit up straight.***

sit up 坐起來；坐直

straight〔stret〕*adv.* 筆直地；挺直地

【比較1】 Sit up. (坐直。)【一般語氣】

Sit up straight. (坐直。)【語氣較強】

當學生在課堂上坐姿不好，趴在桌上，老師就可以說：Sit up. 或 Sit up straight.

【比較2】 Sit up straight. (坐直。)

Stand up straight. (站直。)

老師在課堂上，看到同學坐姿不良，可以說下面這幾句話，我們按照使用頻率排列：

8

① ***Sit up straight.*** (坐直。)【第一常用】

② Please sit up straight. (請坐直。)【第二常用】

③ Everybody sit up straight. (大家坐直。)

④ I want you to sit up straight.
(我要你們坐直。)

⑤ I want everyone to sit up straight.
(我要大家坐直。)

⑥ Sit up straight and pay attention.
(坐直，專心聽。)

⑦ Sit up straight. It's easier to stay alert.
(坐直。這樣比較容易專心。)

【alert〔ə'lɝt〕*adj.* 警覺的；注意的】

9. *Get those shoulders back.*

shoulders〔ˈʃoldɚz〕 *n. pl.* 肩膀

這句話的字面意思是「把那些肩膀放到後面去。」
引申爲「挺胸。」

【比較】

中文：挺胸。

英文：***Get those shoulders back.***

Throw those shoulders back.

Roll those shoulders back.

【*throw back* 使(頭、肩等)向後
roll〔rol〕*v.* 滾動;轉動,當肩膀向後時,
有點像是「轉動」一樣。】

上面三句話的 those shoulders 都可改成 your
shoulders,也可以說:***Get your shoulders
back.*** 這句話和中文思想就有點接近了。

中文所說的「胸」,英文叫作 chest。美國人在
軍隊裡面,常會叫軍人:

Chin in. (收下巴。)

Chest out. (挺胸。)

Stomach in. (縮小腹。)

chin〔tʃɪn〕*n.* 下巴

chest〔tʃɛst〕*n.* 胸部

stomach〔ˈstʌmək〕*n.* 胃;腹部;肚子

8

在軍隊裡，叫士兵挺胸，可說 Chest out. 其他
地方較不適用。在教室裡面，老師常說的三句話是：

Heads up. (抬頭。)
Shoulders back. (挺胸。)
Sit up straight. (坐直。)

Shoulders back. 就是 Get those shoulders
back. 的省略。

當你看到你的朋友彎腰駝背，低著頭在路上
走，你就可以先說：Don't slouch. (不要彎腰駝
背。) 再說下面三句：　　　〔 slautʃ 〕v. 彎腰駝背

Get your head up. (抬頭。)
【對一個人時，不能說 Head up.】
Straighten up. (挺直。)
〔'stretn̩ 〕v. 變直；端正姿勢
Get those shoulders back. (挺胸。)

【對話練習 1】

A：Let's continue.

B：I agree with you.
　　Let's keep going.
　　I don't want to stop.

A：Let's get back to work.

B：Please, not so fast.
　　Wait a few minutes.
　　Let's rest a little longer.

A：Look alive!

B：I'm sorry I'm so tired.
　　Sorry I look sluggish.
　　I didn't sleep well last night.
　　【sluggish〔ˈslʌgɪʃ〕*adj.* 遲緩的】

A：Snap to it!

B：Yes, sir.
　　I'll go faster.
　　I'll speed it up.
　　【*speed up* 加速】

A：我們繼續吧。

B：我同意。
　　我們繼續吧。
　　我不想停下來。

A：我們繼續上課吧。

B：拜託，不要這麼快。
　　再等幾分鐘吧。
　　我們休息久一點吧。

A：要振作起來！

B：抱歉，我很累。
　　抱歉，我看起來懶洋洋的。
　　我昨晚沒睡好。

A：趕快！

B：是的，先生。
　　我會快一點。
　　我會加快速度。

8

【對話練習 2】

A：Show some life.

B：Forgive me.

　　Today's not my day.

　　I'm under the weather today.

　　【*be under the weather* 身體不適】

A：Heads up.

B：Yes, ma'am. 〔mæm〕*n.* 女士

　　I'll pay attention.

　　You have my attention now.

A：Sit up straight.

B：Sorry about that.

　　My posture is bad.

　　　〔'pastʃɚ〕*n.* 姿勢

　　My parents always say that, too.

A：Get those shoulders back.

B：I feel like a soldier.

　　I feel a little taller.

　　This feels pretty good.

　　【soldier〔'soldʒɚ〕*n.* 士兵；軍人

　　　pretty〔'prɪtɪ〕*adv.* 相當】

A：要有精神。

B：原諒我。

　　我今天很倒楣。

　　我今天身體不舒服。

A：頭抬起來。

B：是的，女士。

　　我會專心。

　　我現在很專心。

A：坐直。

B：抱歉。

　　我的姿勢不良。

　　我的父母也常這麼說。

A：挺胸。

B：我覺得像一個軍人。

　　我覺得有比較高一點。

　　這種感覺相當好。

9. *Pay attention.*

Pay attention.
Settle down.
Let's behave.

Stop the chatter.
No talking whatsoever.
No fooling or goofing around.

We're a team.
We're working together.
We're here to accomplish big things.

9

---

attention〔ə'tɛnʃən〕   *pay attention*
settle〔'sɛtl̩〕   *settle down*
behave〔bɪ'hev〕   chatter〔'tʃætɚ〕
whatsoever〔ˌhwɑtso'ɛvɚ〕 *fool around*
goof〔guf〕   *goof around*
team〔tim〕
accomplish〔ə'kɑmplɪʃ〕

【內文解說】

Pay attention.	要專心。
Settle down.	安靜下來。
Let's behave.	我們要守規矩。
Stop the chatter.	不要講個不停。
No talking whatsoever.	絕對不准講話。
No fooling or goofing around.	不要浪費時間胡鬧。
We're a team.	我們是一個團隊。
We're working together.	我們在一起學習。
We're here to accomplish big things.	我們在這裡，要完成大事。

9

** ────────────────

attention〔ə'tɛnʃən〕*n.* 專心；注意　　***pay attention*** 專心
settle〔'sɛtḷ〕*v.* 安定　　***settle down*** 安靜下來
behave〔bɪ'hev〕*v.* 守規矩　　chatter〔'tʃætɚ〕*n.* 喋喋不休
whatsoever〔ˌhwɑtso'ɛvɚ〕*pron.* 無論什麼
fool around 鬼混；遊手好閒；浪費時間 (= *goof around*)
goof〔guf〕*v.* 弄壞；弄糟　　team〔tim〕*n.* 隊；組
work〔wɜk〕*v.* 工作；學習
accomplish〔ə'kɑmplɪʃ〕*v.* 完成

【背景説明】

　　在班上，學生如果講話，老師該怎麼說呢？下
面九句是經過研究後，最佳的選擇。

1. ***Pay attention*.**

attention〔əˋtɛnʃən〕*n.* 注意；專心
pay attention 注意；專心

　　這句話的意思是「要專心。」以下是老師在
課堂上常説的話：

> ***Pay attention*.**（要專心。）【最常用】
> Pay attention to me.【較常用】
> （要專心聽我說。）
> Please pay attention to me.【常用】
> （請專心聽我說。）
>
> Pay attention, everybody.【最常用】
> （大家要專心。）
> Everybody pay attention.【較常用】
> （大家要專心。）
> I want you to pay attention.【常用】
> （我要你們專心聽。）

9

2. *Settle down.*

settle (ˈsɛtl̩) *v.* 安定；安頓；安居
settle down 安靜下來；安定下來

在課堂上，老師除了常說 Be quiet. (安靜。)
　　　　　　　　　　　　(ˈkwaɪət) *adj.* 安靜的
Keep quiet. (保持安靜。) 以外，也常說 ***Settle down.***
意思就是「安靜下來。」例如：Now, children, it's
time to ***settle down*** and start class. (現在，孩子們，
該是你們安靜下來，開始上課的時候了。)

美國老師常說：

> ***Settle down***, class.
> (各位同學，安靜下來。)
> ***Settle down***, guys. 【較常用】
> (各位同學，安靜下來。)
> I want everyone to ***settle down***.
> (我希望大家安靜下來。)

【注意1】 ***Settle down.*** 和 ***Calm down.*** 意義接
近，Calm down. 語氣較強，在課堂
上較少使用。

【例】 ***Calm down.*** Relax. You're out
of control.
(冷靜下來。放輕鬆點。你失去控制了。)

9

【注意2】 美國人常用 *Settle down*. 來勸告單身漢，
要安定下來，有暗示「結婚」的意思。

【例】 You've been single too long. You
should *settle down*.

（你已經單身太久了。你應該結婚了。）

【settle down = get married】

Tom, don't you think it's about time
you *settled down*?

（湯姆，你不覺得現在是你該結婚的時候了嗎？）

【settled down = got married，為什麼用過去式，
詳見「文法寶典」p.374】

3. *Let's behave.*

behave〔bɪ'hev〕v. 舉止端正；守規矩（= *act properly*）

這句話的意思是「我們要守規矩。」相當於
Let's be good. (我們要乖。) 或 Let's be polite.
（我們要有禮貌。）

美國老師常說：

Behave. (要守規矩。)【第二常用】

Behave, please. (請守規矩。)【第三常用】

Everybody **behave**. 【第四常用】
（大家要守規矩。）

Let's behave. (我們要守規矩。)【最常用】

I want you to **behave**. (我要你們守規矩。)【第五常用】

I want everyone to **behave**. 【第六常用】
（我要大家守規矩。）

9

【比較1】　Behave. (要守規矩。)【語氣較強】

　　　　　Let's behave. (我們要守規矩。)

　　　　　【老師說這句話，雖然是包含自己在內，事實上，
　　　　　只是客氣地表示，要同學守規矩。】

【比較2】　behave 是及物和不及物兩用動詞。

　　　　　Behave. (要守規矩。)【較常用】

　　　　　Behave yourselves. (你們要守規矩。)

　　　　　【語氣較強，較少使用，只有小學老師才說。】

【比較3】　behave 的名詞是 behavior (行為)。

　　　　　Let's behave.【較常用】

　　　　　Let's be on our best behavior.【較少用】

　　　　　(我們要很守規矩。)

4. *Stop the chatter.*

chatter〔ˈtʃætɚ〕*n.* 喋喋不休

　　　這句話字面的意思是「停止喋喋不休。」也就
是「不要講個不停。」下面是美國老師在課堂上常
說的話，我們按照使用頻率排列：

① *Stop the chatter.* (不要講個不停。)【最常用】
② Stop the chatter, everybody. 【第二常用】
　　(大家不要講個不停。)
③ Please stop the chatter.
　　(請不要講個不停。)

④ Stop the chatter right now. (立刻停止講話。)

⑤ Stop the chatter and be quiet.

  (不要講個不停，要安靜。)

⑥ Stop the chatter and pay attention.

  (不要講個不停，要專心。)

 Stop the + N. 表「禁止～；不要～。」

= Stop + V-ing.

= No + V-ing.

【例 1 】 ***Stop the chatter.*** (不要講個不停。)

   = Stop chattering.

   = No chattering.

【例 2 】 Stop the talk. (不要講話。)

   = Stop talking.

   = No talking.

【例 3 】 Stop the chat. (不要聊天。)

   = Stop chatting.

   = No chatting.

9

5. *No talking whatsoever.*

 whatsoever〔͵hwɑtso'ɛvɚ〕*pron.* 無論什麼 (= *no matter what*)

  這句話的字面意思是「無論什麼都不能談。」引申爲「絕對不准講話。」等於 No talking at all. 或 No talking no matter what.

  No + V-ing 表「禁止～」，在所有的中外字典上，都寫著 whatsoever 是 whatever 的強調形，但是，在「No + V-ing」，或「No + 名詞」後，只能用 whatsoever 來

加強語氣，此時，whatsoever 是代名詞，只有在意義上等於 whatever，用法上不能互換。【見 The American Heritage Dictionary p.1956】

【例1】　No talking **whatsoever**.【正】
（絕對不准講話。）
No talking whatever.【誤】

【例2】　No food or drinks **whatsoever**.【正】
（嚴禁飲食。）
No food or drinks whatever.【誤】

美國老師在課堂上常説：

No talking whatsoever.（絕對不准講話。）【常用】
No talking, guys.（大家不准講話。）【最常用】
No talking while I'm talking, please.【常用】
（我在講話時，請勿講話。）

No talking!（不准交談！）【較常用】
No talking, please.（請勿講話。）【最常用】
No talking in class.（上課時不准講話。）【較常用】

6. *No fooling or goofing around.*

　　goof〔guf〕的主要意思是「笨蛋」、「白痴」，和 fool 意義相同，當動詞時的意思是「弄糟」、「搞壞」。fool around 和 goof around 同義，意思是「鬼混；遊手好閒；閒蕩；浪費時間」。*No fooling and goofing around.* 的意思是「不要浪費時間胡鬧。」

美國人常說：Get busy.　Stop fooling around.
意思是「找點事情做。不要遊手好閒。」Stop
fooling around. 和 Stop goofing around. 及 Stop
goofing off. 意思完全相同。

【比較】下面三句話意義相同：

No fooling around.【最常用，一般語氣】
（不要浪費時間胡鬧。）
No goofing around.【常用，一般語氣】
（不要浪費時間胡鬧。）
No fooling or goofing around.【語氣最強】
（不要浪費時間胡鬧。）

美國人常將意義相同的單字、片語，甚至句子
放在一起，來加強語氣。

美國小孩常跟爸媽說：

I won't fool around.（我不會浪費時間。）
I won't goof around.（我不會鬼混。）
I will study hard.（我會用功讀書。）

9

7. *We're a team.*

team〔tim〕*n.* 隊；組
（ = *group of people working together*）

這句話的意思是「我們是一個團隊。」美國人
非常講究團隊精神（team spirit），你可以常常和
朋友說這句話，表示你和他的關係很密切。

【比較】 ***We're a team.*** 【一般語氣】
　　　　We're on the same team. 【語氣較強】
　　　　（我們是在同一個團隊。）
　　　　We're all part of the same team. 【語氣最強】
　　　　（我們都是團隊的一份子。）

　　　有老師問道，爲什麼 We're 後面可接 a team? are 是複數動詞，後面不是應該接複數名詞嗎？事實上，在句意合理的情況下，**動詞應和主詞一致，和補語無關**。如：Chinese ***are a*** peace-loving people.（中國人是個愛好和平的民族。）
〔'pipl〕*n.* 民族

8. *We're working together.*

work〔wɜk〕*v.* 工作；學習

　　　這句話字面的意思是「我們在一起工作。」在課堂上，引申爲「我們在一起學習。」也可以加強語氣説成：We're working together to achieve a common goal.（我們在一起學習，以便達成共同的目標。）

9. *We're here to accomplish big things.*

accomplish〔ə'kɑmplɪʃ〕*v.* 完成；實現；達到
big thing 大事；重要的事情（= *important thing*）

　　　這句話的意思是「我們在這裡，要完成大事。」big things 也可説成 great things。

【對話練習 1】

A：Pay attention.

B：I'm sorry.

Forgive me.

It won't happen again.

A：Let's behave.

B：We're sorry.

We'll behave.

We promise to behave.

A：Stop the chatter.

B：Sorry about that.

We'll be quiet.

You won't hear another word.

A：No talking whatsoever.

B：I understand.

No talking allowed.

I won't say a word.

A：要專心。

B：很抱歉。

原諒我。

這種事不會再發生了。

A：我們要守規矩。

B：我們很抱歉。

我們會守規矩。

我們保證會守規矩。

A：不要講個不停。

B：很抱歉。

我們會安靜。

你不會聽到我們再說半句話。

A：絕對不准講話。

B：我知道。

不准講話。

我不會說半句話。

9

【對話練習 2】

A：No fooling or goofing around.   A：不要浪費時間鬼混。

B：That's a good rule.   B：那是個好規定。
　　No fooling around in class.   　　上課時要專心。
　　Every student must pay attention.   　　每個學生都必須專心。

A：We're a team.   A：我們是一個團隊。

B：I totally agree.   B：我完全同意。
　　This class is a team.   　　這一班是個團隊。
　　Every student is part of the team.   　　每個學生都是團隊的
　　【totally〔'totḷ〕adv. 完全地】   　　一份子。

A：We're working together.   A：我們正在一起努力。

B：I'm glad to hear that.   B：我很高興聽到這句話。
　　Let's cooperate.   　　我們合作吧。
　　Let's help each other out.   　　我們互相幫忙吧。
　　【cooperate〔ko'ɑpə,ret〕v. 合作
　　　help sb. out 幫助某人脫離困境】

A：We're here to accomplish big   A：我們在這裡，要完成
　　things.   　　大事。

B：I feel the same way.   B：我有同感。
　　Learning English is so   　　學英文很重要。
　　important.
　　It is my number one goal.   　　它是我的第一目標。
　　【goal〔gol〕n. 目標】

10. Write out the lesson.

Write out the lesson.
Write it from memory.
Write it down word for word.

Make sure you print.
Make it look neat.
Don't scribble.

Take your time.
Get it right.
Do a good job.

10

---

write out	lesson ('lɛsn̩)
memory ('mɛmərɪ)	*from memory*
write down	*word for word*
make sure	print (prɪnt)
neat (nit)	scribble ('skrɪbl̩)
take one's time	

【內文解說】

Write out the lesson.	把這一課全部寫出來。
Write it from memory.	把它默寫下來。
Write it down word for word.	把它一字不差地寫下來。
Make sure you print.	你們一定要用印刷體寫。
Make it look neat.	要寫整齊。
Don't scribble.	不要寫得太潦草。
Take your time.	慢慢來。
Get it right.	好好做。
Do a good job.	好好做；要做好。

10

** ————————————————

write out 全部寫出　　lesson〔'lɛsn̩〕*n.* 課
memory〔'mɛmərɪ〕*n.* 記憶；記憶力
from memory 憑記憶　　*write down* 寫下來
word for word 一字不差地　　*make sure* 確定
print〔prɪnt〕*v.* 用印刷體書寫　　neat〔nit〕*adj.* 整齊的
scribble〔'skrɪbl̩〕*v.* 寫潦草的字
take one's time 慢慢來；不急

【背景説明】

美國老師很少叫同學默寫文章，所以，「默寫」這兩個字，往往連美國人都搞不清楚。事實上，默寫有助於記憶，默寫一遍，等於看七遍。老師可以叫同學默寫「一口氣英語」，作爲考試。

1. *Write out the lesson.*
   write out （不省略地）全部寫出
   lesson〔ˈlɛsn̩〕*n.* 課

   這句話的意思是「把這一課全部寫出來。」也可以説成：Write out the text.（把課文全部寫出來。）
   〔tɛkst〕*n.* 課文

   【比較1】 *Write out the lesson.*【正，較常用】
   　　　　 Write the lesson out.【正，較少用】

   【比較2】 Write it out.【正，較常用】
   　　　　 （把它全部寫出來。）
   　　　　 Write out it.【誤】

   【比較3】 write out 和 write down 意思不同，write out 是「全部寫出來」，write down 是「寫下來」。

   　　　　 Write out the lesson.
   　　　　 （把這一課全部寫出來。）
   　　　　 Write down the lesson.
   　　　　 （把這一課寫下來。）

10

美國老師常説：

Write out the lesson. 【第一常用】
Please write out the lesson. 【第六常用】
（請把這一課全部寫出來。）
Please write out the text. 【常用】
（請把課文全部寫出來。）

Write the lesson out. 【第二常用】
（把這一課全部寫出來。）
Write the whole lesson out. 【第三常用】
（把整課全部寫出來。）
I want you to write out the lesson. 【第四常用】
（我要你們把這一課全部寫出來。）

Write it out. （把它全部寫出來。）【常用】
Write it all out. （把它全部寫出來。）【常用】
Write everything out. 【常用】
（把每樣東西都寫出來。）

Please write it out. 【第五常用】
（請把它全部寫出來。）
You must write it out. 【較不常用】
（你們必須把它全部寫出來。）

10

2. *Write it from memory.*
memory〔ˈmɛmərɪ〕*n.* 記憶；記憶力
from memory 憑記憶

這句話字面的意思是「憑記憶把它寫下來。」
引申為「把它默寫下來。」

也可以說成：

Write it down from memory.
（把它默寫下來。）
Write it out from memory.
（把它全部默寫出來。）
Write it all out from memory.
（把它全部默寫出來。）

老師說 *Write it from memory.* 的涵義是叫
同學 Don't copy it.（不要抄。）Don't look
at the book.（不要看書。）

10

3. *Write it down word for word.*
write down 寫下來（ = *put down* = *get down* ）
word for word 一字不差地

一般成語字典上，不容易找到 word for
word 這個成語，但是在 "A Dictionary of
American Idioms"（ p.452 ），有最好的解釋：
in exactly the same words（一字不差地）。

【比較】 word for word 和 word by word 不同：

I memorized the speech *word for word*.
（這篇演講的每一個字，我都背下來了。）

You're speaking too fast. Say it *word by word*. （你說得太快了。一個字一個字地說。）

【*word by word* 一個字一個字地 (= *one word at a time*)】

Write it down word for word. 的意思是
「把它一字不差地寫下來。」

也有美國老師說成：

Please write it down *word for word*.
（請把它一字不差地寫下來。）

I want you to write it down *word for word*.
（我要你們把它一字不差地寫下來。）

Write it down on paper *word for word*.
〔'pepɚ 〕*n.* 考卷
（把它全部寫在考卷上。）【「一字不差地」意思就是「全部」】

Write it down. （把它寫下來。）
Write it all down. （把它全部寫下來。）
Write it down on paper. （把它寫在考卷上。）

write 可用 put 或 get 來代替，Write it down. 也可
說成：Put it down. 或 Get it down. 使用頻率幾乎
相同。

4. *Make sure you print.*

   make sure 確定

   print〔prɪnt〕v. 用印刷體書寫

      make sure 源自 make sure of 這個成語，由於 that 子句不能做介詞的受詞，故 of 省略掉。所以，

Make sure (that) + 子句

【that 子句做受詞時，that 常省略。】

【比較】*Make sure you print.*【正，常用，通俗】

        （你們一定要用印刷體寫。）

        Make sure that you print.【正，較少使用】

Make sure + 子句，很常用，如：

   Make sure you have enough money with you.

   （你身上一定要有足夠的錢。）

   Make sure you can be there.

   （要確定你能到那裡。）

   Make sure you can make a reservation.

   （要確定你能夠訂到位子。）〔͵rɛzɚˋveʃən〕n. 預訂

下面是美國老師在課堂上常說的話：

   Make sure you print.【第一常用】

   （你們一定要用印刷體寫。）

   Please make sure you print.【第五常用】

   （請你們一定要用印刷體寫。）

   I want you to make sure you print.

   （我要你們一定要用印刷體寫。）【第四常用】

10

Don't write. Make sure you print.
（不要用草寫。一定要用印刷體寫。）【第六常用】
【此時的 write 是指「草寫」。】
You must print. 【第二常用】
（你們必須用印刷體寫。）
I want you to print. 【第三常用】
（我要你們用印刷體寫。）

很多美國人喜歡草寫，所以，不管是填公文或任何表格，上面都會註明：Print in capital letters.（用印刷體大寫字母書寫。）為什麼不用小寫的印刷體呢？因為小寫的 i 和 l 很接近，i 上常忘了點一點，r 和 v 或 a 和 o 也很接近。一般考試，老師要求同學用印刷體，則是和課本一樣，該大寫就大寫，該小寫就小寫。

5. *Make it look neat.*

neat〔nit〕*adj.* 整潔的；工整的；整齊的

10

這句話的字面意思是「使它看起來整齊。」在這裡可引申為「要寫整齊。」這和中文思想不同。

【比較1】 ***Make it look neat.*** 【正，常用】
Make it neat. （寫整齊。）【正，常用】
Write it neatly. 【正】
（寫整齊；草寫整齊。）
在課堂上單獨說 Write it neatly. 這句話，學生可能會誤會成，可用他自己的方式寫整齊，也許是用印刷體，也許是草寫。

【比較 2】 中文： 用印刷體寫整齊。

英文： Print neatly.【正，常用】

Print it neatly.【正，常用】

下面是美國老師在課堂上常說的話，我們按
照使用頻率排列：

① Make it neat.【第一常用】

② ***Make it look neat.***【第二常用】

③ Make it look really neat.（要寫得很整齊。）

④ You must make it look neat.
（你們必須把它寫整齊。）

⑤ I want you to make it look neat.
（我要你們把它寫整齊。）

⑥ I want everyone to make it look neat.
（我要大家把它寫整齊。）

6. *Don't scribble.*

scribble〔'skrɪbl̩〕 *v.* 寫潦草的字（= *write carelessly*）

10

這句話字面的意思是「不要寫潦草的字。」
可引申為「不要寫得太潦草。」或「寫清楚。」
（= *Write clearly.*）

美國老師常說：

Write carefully.（小心寫。）

Write neatly.（寫整齊。）

Don't scribble.（不要寫得太潦草。）

在中文裡，說「不要寫得太潦草。」意思是叫你「寫整齊。」並不是說可以寫得有點潦草。中文說這句話，是有一點禮貌的語氣，但是，在英文中並沒有。所以美國人不說：*Don't scribble too much.*（誤）他們只說：Don't scribble. 或 Don't scribble at all.（不要寫得亂七八糟。）

7. *Take your time.*

take *one's* **time** 慢慢來；不急

這句話的意思是「慢慢來。」美國人常常使用。美國老師也常說：

You can take your time.（你們可以慢慢來。）
Everybody take your time.（大家慢慢來。）
I want you to take your time.
（我希望你們慢慢來。）
【want 在此作「希望」解。】

10

叫別人「慢慢來。」的說法很多：

Take your time.（慢慢來。）【第一常用】
Don't rush.（不急。）【第四常用】
Don't hurry.（不急。）【第五常用】

Don't be in a rush.（不要急。）【第八常用】
Don't be in a hurry.（不要急。）【第九常用】

There's no rush. (不急。)【第二常用】
There's no hurry. (不急。)【第三常用】

You don't have to rush. 【第六常用】
(你們不需要急。)
You don't have to hurry. 【第七常用】
(你們不需要急。)
【rush〔 rʌʃ 〕*v. n.* 匆忙   hurry〔'hɜɪ 〕*v. n.* 匆忙】

8. *Get it right.*

字典上找不到這句話，但是美國人常說，
意思是「好好做。」等於 Do it right. 或 Do it
correctly. Don't make a mistake. (不要犯錯。)
〔 kə'rɛktlɪ 〕*adv.* 正確地

【例】 *Get it right* the first time.
(第一次就要好好做。)
He is very able. He always *gets it right*.
〔'ebl 〕*adj.* 有能力的
(他很有能力，他做事的方法總是很正確。)
You are the one who always *gets it right*.
(你做事的方法總是很正確。)

美國老師在課堂上，還常說：

Please *get it right*. (請好好做。)
You must *get it right*. (你們必須好好做。)
I want you to *get it right*.
(我要你們好好做。)

10

【比較】 *Get it right*. (好好做。)

　　　　Get it done right. (好好做完。)

　　Get it right. 的意思是「好好做。」(= *Do it correctly.*) 是指方法。而 Get it done right. 也可以加強語氣說成：Get it done the right way. 或 Get it done using the right way. 意思都是「要好好把它做完。」有強調「好好做完」的意味。

9. *Do a good job*.

　　事情尚未做以前，老師常說這句話來鼓勵同學，叫他們「好好做。」或「要做好。」在考試前說這句話，意思就是「好好考試。」或「要考好。」發成績單的時候，學生考得不錯，老師就會說：You did a good job. (你考得很好。) 或只說 Good job.

　　這類的說法有：

Do a good job. (好好做。)【最常用】
Do a great job. (好好做。)【最常用】
Do a super job. (要好好做。)【較常用】
　〔'supɚ〕 *adj.* 極佳的

Do an excellent job. (要好好做。)【較常用】
　〔'ɛkslənt〕 *adj.* 極佳的
Do the best you can do. (儘量做好。)【常用】
Do a job you can be proud of. 【常用】
　(要做好到你能夠引以爲榮。)【*be proud of* 以…爲榮】

10

Do your best. (盡力做好。)【最常用】

Do your very best. (盡力做好。)【較常用】

Do the best you can. 【較常用】

(盡你們最大的力量做好。)

在考試前，老師還常說：

Please do a good job. 【第一常用】

(請好好做。)

Make sure you do a good job. 【第五常用】

(你們一定要好好做。)

I want you to do a good job. 【第二常用】

(我希望你們好好做。)

Everybody do a good job. 【第三常用】

(大家好好做。)

I expect everybody to do a good job.

(我希望你們好好做。)【第六常用】

【expect 主要意思是「期望」，在此作「希望」解。】

Do a good job on it. 【第四常用】

(這件事要好好做。)

【Please do a good job. 在考試時，就可翻成

「請好好考試。」】

10

【比較】 ***Do a good job.***
   Get it right.

Do a good job. 有兩個意思：①好好做。(= *Do it correctly.*)【指「方法」】②要做好。(= *Do quality work.*)【指「把工作做好」】

Get it right. 意思是「好好做。」只是指「方法」，等於 Do it correctly.

10. 補充說明

這一回的最後三句：***Take your time. Get it right. Do a good job.*** 可以用在很多場合。

老師在考試前說這些話，可讓同學感覺輕鬆一點。老板也可以對員工說這些話，叫他們慢慢做，把事情做好。家長交待小孩做一件事時，也可以說這三句話，叫他們放輕鬆，不要急，好好做。

10

【對話練習 1】

A：Write out the lesson.

B：That's not a problem.
I'm ready to do it.
I have been practicing.

A：Write it from memory.

B：That's a challenge.
That's tough to do.
That's not an easy task.
【 challenge 〔'tʃælɪndʒ 〕 *n.* 挑戰
tough 〔 tʌf 〕 *adj.* 困難的
task 〔 tæsk 〕 *n.* 任務；工作 】

A：Write it down word for word.

B：Don't worry.
I'll do it all.
I won't miss a thing.
【 do 〔 du 〕 *v.* 寫
miss 〔 mɪs 〕 *v.* 漏掉；省略 】

A：Make sure you print.

B：I'll print each word.
I'll print every letter.
I won't write in cursive style.
【 letter 〔'lɛtɚ 〕 *n.* 字母
cursive 〔'kɝsɪv 〕 *adj.* 草寫的 】

A：把這一課全部寫出來。

B：沒問題。
我準備好要寫了。
我一直有在練習。

A：把它默寫下來。

B：那是一項挑戰。
那很困難。
那並不容易。

A：把它一字不差地寫下來。

B：別擔心。
我會全部寫下來。
我不會漏掉任何東西。

A：你一定要用印刷體寫。

B：我每個字都會用印刷體寫。
我每個字母都會用印刷體寫。
我不會寫草寫體。

10

【對話練習 2】

A：Don't scribble.

B：Don't worry, I won't.
I'll be careful.
You can count on me.
【*count on* 信賴】

A：不要寫得太潦草。

B：別擔心，我不會的。
我會小心的。
你可以信賴我。

A：Take your time.

B：I appreciate that.
I need some time.
I hate to hurry things.
【appreciate〔əˈpriʃɪˌet〕v. 感激
hurry〔ˈhɝɪ〕v. 匆促地做】

A：慢慢來。

B：我很感激。
我需要一些時間。
我討厭匆促地做事情。

A：Get it right.

B：I totally understand.
〔ˈtotḷɪ〕*adv.* 完全地
I know what you want.
I'll get it right.

A：好好做。

B：我完全了解。

我知道你要什麼。
我會好好做。

10

A：Do a good job.

B：I'll do a good job.
I'll give it my all.
I won't let you down.
【*give it one's all* 盡力
let sb. down 讓某人失望】

A：好好做。

B：我會好好做。
我會盡力。
我不會讓你失望。

11. *Time's up.*

Time's up.
That's it for now.
That's all for today.

Class is over.
Class dismissed.
Don't forget your assignment.

Memorize the lesson.
Learn it by heart.
Be ready for a quiz.

11

up〔ʌp〕   *for now*
over〔'ovɚ〕   dismiss〔dɪs'mɪs〕
assignment〔ə'saɪnmənt〕
memorize〔'mɛmə,raɪz〕
by heart   quiz〔kwɪz〕

【內文解説】

Time's up.	時間到了。
That's it for now.	現在到此為止。
That's all for today.	今天到此為止。
Class is over.	課程結束了。
Class dismissed.	下課。
Don't forget your assignment.	不要忘記你的家庭作業。
Memorize the lesson.	把這一課背好。
Learn it by heart.	把它背下來。
Be ready for a quiz.	好好準備小考。

11

** ————————————————————

up〔ʌp〕*adv.* 完畢;到期　　*for now* 目前;暫時
over〔'ovɚ〕*adv.* 完畢;結束
dismiss〔dɪs'mɪs〕*v.* 解散;下(課);讓…離開
assignment〔ə'saɪnmənt〕*n.* (給學生的)指定作業或功課
memorize〔'mɛmə,raɪz〕*v.* 記住;背熟
by heart 靠記憶　　quiz〔kwɪz〕*n.* 小考;隨堂測驗

【背景説明】

老師要結束今天課程的時候，就可先説這九句話，熱身一下。

1. **Time's up.**

up〔ʌp〕*adv.* 完畢；到期

up 的主要意思是「向上」，源自時針向上，指到十二點鐘，是指時間的結束 (the end of the hour)。所以，**Time's up.** 的意思是「時間到了。」up 指「完畢」或「到期」，像：When is your contract up? (你的合約什麼時候到期？)　〔ˈkɑntrækt〕*n.* 合約

Time's up. 這句話可以加長。看看下面六句，很有意思，都是美國老師常説的話，我們按照使用頻率排列，剛好是由短到長：

① **Time's up.** (時間到了。)【第一常用】
② Our time is up. (我們的時間到了。)【第二常用】
③ Class time is up. (上課時間結束了。)

11

④ Our class time is up. (我們的上課時間結束了。)
⑤ Our class time for today is up.
　　(我們今天的上課時間結束了。)
⑥ Our class time for today is almost up.
　　(我們今天的上課時間差不多要結束了。)

下面六句話，美國老師也常說，我們按照使用頻率排列：

① It's time. (時間到了。)【第一常用】

② It's time to stop. (停止的時間到了。)【第二常用】

③ It's time to quit. (該停止的時間到了。)
〔 kwɪt 〕*v.* 停止

④ I'm afraid time is up. (恐怕時間到了。)

⑤ Time is almost up. (時間差不多到了。)

⑥ Time is about up. (時間差不多到了。)

Time's up. 這麼簡單的句子，卻有這麼多的表達方法。你看看，說英文多有趣。「一口氣英語」背熟以後，你自然就可以說出美國人講的話，因為我們已經把美國人所說的話，最精華的部份，全部都提供給你了。

2. ***That's it for now.***

for now 目前；暫時

11

美國人常說 ***That's it.*** 字面的意思是「那個是它。」在不同的句子中，有不同的解釋，所有的字典上都沒寫清楚，看看下面的例句，你就知道它真正的涵義了。

【例1】 ***That's it.*** It's right there. It's on the table. (就是那個。就在那裡。它就在桌子上。)
【That's it. 是字面的意思，it 指「東西」(object)。】

【例2】 ***That's it.*** That's right. That's exactly
what I want.

（那就是了。對了。那正是我要的。）

【That's it. = That's right. = That's correct.】

【例3】 ***That's it*** for me. I've had enough.
I ate too much.

（夠了，我吃飽了。我吃太多了。）

【That's it. = That's enough. = No more.】

【例4】 ***That's it.*** I've had enough. I'm very
upset. （好了，我受夠了。我很生氣。）

〔ʌpˈsɛt〕*adj.* 生氣的

【That's it. 也可用在生氣時，等於 That's enough.】

從上面例句，我們可以很清楚知道，That's it.
有三個主要意思：①就是那個。②對了。③夠了。

for now 字面的意思是「對於現在」，引申為
「目前」或「現在（暫時）」。***That's it for now.***
字面的意思「現在夠了。」在此引申為「現在到此
為止。」(= *That's enough for now.*)

在課堂上，老師常說：

> ***That's it for now.*** 【最常用】
> （現在到此為止。）
>
> That's it for today. 【最常用】
> （今天到此為止。）
>
> That's it. （到此為止。）【最常用】

11

That's it for class today.【較常用】

（今天的課到此為止。）

That's it for today's class.【較常用】

（今天的課到此為止。）

That's it for today's lesson.【常用】

（今天的課程到此為止。）

【一般說來，lesson 和 class 意思相同，都可
以表示「課程」，但是，one class（一堂課）
也許有好幾個 lesson。】

That's it. 可以和其他的句子一起說。如：

That's it. We are finished.

（好了，我們結束了。）

We've covered the whole lesson. ***That's
it*** for today.

（我們已經上完整課了。今天到此為止。）

We are done. ***That's it*** for today's class.

（我們上完了。今天的課到此為止。）

【cover〔ˈkʌvɚ〕v. 涵蓋；講課
　done〔dʌn〕adj. 完成的；結束的】

11

3. *That's all for today.*

這句話字面的意思是「對於今天，那是全部。」
引申為「今天到此為止。」

【比較】***That's all for today***.【正】

That's all today.【誤】

today 是副詞，在文法上，沒有錯，但這個句子
美國人不說，因為沒有意義，你不能說「今天那
是全部。」你只能說「對於今天，那是全部。」

美國老師在課堂上常説：

That's all. (到此爲止。)【第三常用】

That's all for today. (今天到此爲止。)【最常用】

That's all for now. (現在到此爲止。)【第二常用】

That's all we have to do. 【第八常用】
（ 我們必須做的，就那麼多了。）

That's all we need to do. 【第七常用】
（ 那是我們必須做的。）

That's all for today's class. 【第四常用】
（ 今天的課到此爲止。）

That's all we are doing for today. 【第五常用】
（ 我們今天必須做的，到此爲止。）

That's all we are going to do. 【第六常用】
（ 我們要做的，到此爲止。）

4. ***Class is over.***

over〔'ovə〕*adv.* 結束；完畢（ = *ended* ; *finished* ）

這句話的意思是「課程結束了。」

美國老師常説：

Class is over. (課程結束了。)【最常用】

This class is over. (這一節課結束了。)【最常用】

Today's class is over. 【最常用】
（ 今天的課程結束了。）

11

Class is over for today.【較常用】
（今天的課程結束了。）
Our class is over for today.【較常用】
（我們今天的課程結束了。）
Our class is over.【常用】
（我們的課程結束了。）

Our time is up. (我們的時間到了。)【較常用】
Class is finished. (我們上完課了。)【常用】
We're finished. (我們上完了。)【常用】
【We're finished. 和 We're done. 爲什麼用被動？
詳見「一口氣英語②」p.10–3 , 10–4】

5. ***Class dismissed.***

dismiss〔dɪs'mɪs〕*v.* 解散；下（課）；讓…離開

這句話源自：Class is dismissed. 意思是
「下課。」***Class dismissed.*** 省略 is 後，已經
變成慣用句了。

【比較1】***Class dismissed.*** 【正，有命令語氣，較常用】
Class is dismissed. 【正，少用】

美國老師也常説：

Class is over. You're dismissed.
（課程結束了。你們可以走了。）
This class is over. You are dismissed.
（這堂課結束了。你們可以走了。）
Class is over. Everyone is dismissed.
（課程結束了。大家解散。）

11

【比較 2 】 *Class dismissed.*【正，慣用句，動詞 is 省略】
　　　　　This class dismissed.
　　　　　【誤，不是慣用句，is 不可省略，應改成：
　　　　　This class is dismissed.】

6. *Don't forget your assignment.*

assignment〔ə'saɪnmənt〕*n.* (給學生的) 指定作業或功課

　　assign 是「指派」的意思，assignment 是「指派的工作」，可能是老板或老師所指派的工作，在課堂上，等於 homework。這句話的意思是「不要忘記你的家庭作業。」(= *Don't forget your homework.*)

　　美國老師常說：

Don't forget your assignment.【最常用】
(不要忘記你的家庭作業。)
Don't forget your assignment for today.
(不要忘記你今天的家庭作業。)【第六常用】
Don't forget today's assignment.【第二常用】
(不要忘記今天的家庭作業。)

Do your homework. (要做功課。)【第五常用】
Remember your homework.【第三常用】
(要記得做功課。)
Remember to do your homework.【第四常用】
(要記得做你的功課。)

11

7. *Memorize the lesson.*

memorize〔'mɛmə,raɪz〕*v.* 熟記；記住；背熟

很多字典把 memorize 翻成「記憶」或「背誦」，事實上，memorize 的意思是「背好」，等於 learn by heart。這句話的意思是「把這一課背好。」

【比較 1】

中文： 把這一課背好。

英文： *Memorize the lesson.*【常用】

Learn the lesson by heart.【常用】

Commit the lesson to memory.【正，少用】

【*commit sth. to memory*「記住某事」，這句話是書本英文，美國人不說。】

【比較 2】 memorize 和 recite 意思完全不同：

英文： *Memorize the lesson.*（把這一課背好。）

Recite the lesson.（把這一課背出來。）

【recit〔rɪ'saɪt〕*v.* 朗誦；背誦（= *say it from memory*）】

下面的句子，美國老師常說：

Memorize today's lesson.【第二常用】

（把今天的課程背好。）

·Memorize what we learned.【第四常用】

（把我們所學的背好。）

Memorize what we did today.【第五常用】

（把我們今天所學的背好。）

11

Memorize the text. 【最常用】
（把課文背好。）
Memorize today's text. 【第六常用】
（把今天的課文背好。）
Memorize everything from today. 【第三常用】
（把今天學的所有東西都背好。）

8. *Learn it by heart.*

by heart 靠記憶

by heart 常和動詞 get, learn, say, recite, know 等連用。

Learn it by heart. 字面的意思是「用心學習它。」引申為「把它背下來。」可能源自於心臟是自動跳的，背熟了就可以自動說出來，不要思考。

中文： 把「一口氣英語」背下來。
英文： Learn *One Breath English* by heart.

中文： 把這篇演講稿背下來。
英文： Learn the speech by heart.

中文： 把這一課背下來。
英文： Learn the lesson by heart.

11

9. ***Be ready for a quiz.***
   be ready for 為～做好準備
   quiz〔kwɪz〕*n.* 小考；隨堂測驗

   　　quiz 是「小考」，test 是「一般考試」，exam 是「大考」。在美國，幾乎每次上課，老師都會考小考（quiz），每個單元就會有一次考試（test），到了期中，有期中考（mid-term exam），學期結束，有期末考（final exam）。美國人只有在書寫時才用 examination。

   　　Be ready for a quiz. 意思是「好好準備小考。」

   　　中國人一般只說「好好準備考試。」並不指明「小考」，看看下面比較就知道：

   【比較】
   　中文： 好好準備考試。
   　英文： ① ***Be ready for a quiz.***

   　　　　在這句話中，所指的「考試」，是一般隨堂考，老師未必會考，通常是用來嚇唬學生，為了讓同學回家複習功課。

   　　　　② Be ready for a test.
   　　　　test 是件大事，美國老師通常在一兩週前就會告訴同學，不會臨時通知要考試，他們通常會說：

   Be ready for a test next Friday.
   （好好準備下禮拜五的考試。）

   Be ready for a test on the material next week.　〔mə'tɪrɪəl〕*n.* 教材
   （好好準備下禮拜這份教材的考試。）

【對話練習 1】

A：Time's up.

B：That was fast!
Time really flies!
Time flies when you're
having fun.
【 fly〔flaɪ〕*v.*（時間）飛也似地
過去 *have fun* 玩得愉快】

A：That's it for now.

B：Thank God.
I'm tired out.
I'm glad we're stopping.
【*be tired out* 累壞了】

A：That's all for today.

B：That's too bad.
I hate to stop.
I enjoy doing this.

A：Class dismissed.

B：Thank you.
That was interesting.
I really enjoyed today's class.

A：時間到了。

B：真是快！
時間真的過得很快！
正玩得愉快時，時間過得
很快。

A：現在到此爲止。

B：謝天謝地。
我累壞了。
很高興我們要停止了。

A：今天到此爲止。

B：真糟糕。
我真不願意停下來。
我喜歡做這個。

A：下課。

B：謝謝。
那很有趣。
我真的很喜歡上今天的課。

11

【對話練習 2】

A：Don't forget your assignment.　　A：不要忘記你的家庭作業。

B：I won't forget.　　　　　　　　 B：我不會忘記的。
　　I wrote it down.　　　　　　　　 我把它寫下來了。
　　I know it's very important.　　　 我知道它很重要。

A：Memorize the lesson.　　　　　　A：把這一課背好。

B：I already did.　　　　　　　　　 B：我已經背好了。
　　I memorized it all.　　　　　　　 我全都背好了。
　　I know it all by heart.　　　　　　 我全都背下來了。

A：Learn it by heart.　　　　　　　　A：把它背下來。

B：That's good advice.　　　　　　　B：那是很好的建議。
　　That's the best way to learn.　　 那是最好的學習方式。
　　I memorize every lesson.　　　　 我每一課都會背。
　　【advice〔əd'vaɪs〕*n.* 忠告；建議】

A：Be ready for a quiz.　　　　　　　A：好好準備小考。

B：Thanks for the warning.　　　　　B：謝謝你的警告。
　　I'll be ready.　　　　　　　　　 我會準備好的。
　　I'll be prepared for a quiz.　　　 我會好好準備小考。
　　【warning〔'wɔrnɪŋ〕*n.* 警告】

12. Great work today.

Great work today.
Great effort, everybody.
You did a super job.

You're getting better.
You're making progress.
You're on the right track.

You make me proud.
You guys are the best.
I want to thank you all.

---

great〔gret〕
super〔'supɚ,'sju-〕
progress〔'prɑgrɛs,'pro-〕
track〔træk〕
proud〔praʊd〕

effort〔'ɛfɚt〕
make progress
on the right track
guy〔gaɪ〕

12

【內文解說】

Great work today.	你們今天表現得很好。
Great effort, everybody.	你們很努力。
You did a super job.	你們表現得太棒了。
You're getting better.	你們越來越好。
You're making progress.	你們越來越進步了。
You're on the right track.	你們方向正確;你們的做法正確。
You make me proud.	我以你們為榮。
You guys are the best.	你們是最棒的。
I want to thank you all.	我要謝謝大家。

** ———————————————

great〔gret〕*adj.* 很棒的;很大的
effort〔'ɛfət〕*n.* 努力
super〔'supə,'sju-〕*adj.* 極佳的
progress〔'prɑgrɛs,'pro-〕*n.* 進步
make progress 進步　　track〔træk〕*n.* 軌道
on the right track 方向正確;做法、想法正確
proud〔praud〕*adj.* 驕傲的;感到光榮的
guy〔gaɪ〕*n.* 人

12

【背景說明】

老師下課前，可說這九句話來鼓勵同學，上完課後，一定要說一些感人的話再離開，才能顯示出老師的教學熱忱。

1. ***Great work today.***

great〔gret〕*adj.* 很棒的；很大的
work〔wɜk〕*n.* 工作（不可數名詞）

這句話源自 You did great work today. 意思是「你們今天表現得很好。」相當於 Great job today. 這兩句話都一樣常用。

【比較】 You did a great job today.【正】
（你們今天表現得很好。）
You did a great work today.【誤】
【work 不可數，前面不可加冠詞】
You did great work today.【正】
（你們今天表現得很好。）

美國老師在下課前常說：

Great work today.【第一常用】
（你們今天表現得很好。）
You did great today.【第二常用】
（你們今天表現得很好。）
You did great work today.【第三常用】
（你們今天表現得很好。）

12

You did nice work today. 【第七常用】
（你們今天表現得不錯。）
You all did great. 【第四常用】
（你們都表現得很好。）
You all did great work in class today. 【第六常用】
（你們今天在課堂上都表現得很好。）

You all did great work today. 【第五常用】
（你們今天都表現得很好。）
Everyone did great today. 【第八常用】
（大家今天都表現得很好。）
Everyone did really great work today. 【常用】
（大家今天真的都表現得很好。）

Great work today. I'm proud of you. 【常用】
（你們今天表現得很好。我以你們為榮。）
Great work today. Thank you so much. 【常用】
（你們今天表現得很好。非常感謝你們。）

「**Great**＋名詞」是美國人的口頭禪，看完電影後，
說：Great movie.（電影真棒。）天氣很好時說：
Great weather.（天氣真好。）買東西買到好價錢，
可以說 Great price.（價錢真好。）

12

2. *Great effort, everybody.*

   effort〔'ɛfət〕*n.* 努力

      這句話源自：Everybody made a great effort. 意思是「大家很努力。」相當於 You worked very hard.（你們很努力。）

      在文法上，effort 是可數和不可數兩用名詞，但是，美國人很少用 *Great efforts, everybody.* 問了十九位在美國大學任課的老師，只有一位覺得 Great effort 和 Great efforts 都可以。

      下面的話，你都可以在下課前說，我們按照使用頻率排列：

① *Great effort, everybody.*【第一常用】
   （你們很努力。）

② *Great effort,* class.【第二常用】
   （全班同學都很努力。）

③ *Great effort,* everybody. Thank you.【第三常用】
   （你們很努力。謝謝你們。）

④ You worked very hard.（你們很努力。）

⑤ You really studied hard.
   （你們真的很用功。）

⑥ I know everybody made a great effort today.
   （我知道大家今天都很努力。）

12

3. ***You did a super job.***

super〔'supɚ, 'sju- 〕*adj.* 極佳的

這句話的意思是「你們表現得太棒了。」美國人喜歡說這類的話：

You did a ***good*** job.（你們表現得很好。）
You did a ***great*** job.（你們表現得很棒。）
You did a ***super*** job.（你們表現得太棒了。）

You did an ***excellent*** job.（你們表現得很棒。）
You did a ***terrific*** job.（你們表現得很棒。）
You did a ***marvelous*** job.（你們表現得很棒。）

You did a ***fantastic*** job.（你們表現得很棒。）
You did a ***tremendous*** job.（你們表現得很棒。）
You did a ***wonderful*** job.（你們表現得很棒。）

excellent〔'ɛkslənt〕*adj.* 極佳的
terrific〔təˈrɪfɪk〕*adj.* 很棒的
marvelous〔'mɑrvləs〕*adj.* 很棒的
fantastic〔fænˈtæstɪk〕*adj.* 很棒的
tremendous〔trɪˈmɛndəs〕*adj.* 極好的

12

下面的句子語氣較強：

You did a ***perfect*** job.（你們表現得很完美。）
You did a ***remarkable*** job.（你們表現得很傑出。）
You did a ***sensational*** job.（你們表現得棒極了。）

You did an *extraordinary* job.
（你們表現得與眾不同。）
You did an *exceptional* job.（你們表現得太好了。）
You did an *amazing* job.（你們表現得很棒。）

remarkable〔rɪ'mɑrkəbl̩〕*adj.* 非凡的；卓越的
sensational〔sɛn'seʃənl̩〕*adj.* 極好的
extraordinary〔ɪk'strɔrdn̩ˌɛrɪ〕*adj.* 非凡的；令人驚異的
exceptional〔ɪk'sɛpʃənl̩〕*adj.* 特別的；優秀的
amazing〔ə'mezɪŋ〕*adj.* 令人驚訝的

　　下面的話，以 super job 為例，老師也可以
在課堂上說，我們按照使用頻率排列：

① ***You did a super job today.***【第一常用】
　　（你們今天表現得太棒了。）
② You did a super job in class today.【第二常用】
　　（你們今天在課堂上表現得太棒了。）
③ You all did a really super job.
　　（你們表現得真是太棒了。）

④ Super job, everybody.（你們表現得太棒了。）
⑤ Thanks for the super job.
　　（謝謝你們，表現得太棒了。）
⑥ Thanks for doing such a super job.
　　（謝謝你們，表現得這麼棒。）

12

　　　以上句中的 a super job 可改成 a great job
或 an excellent job 等。第四句中的 Super job
可以改成 Great job 或 Excellent job 等。

4. *You're getting better.*

說別人很好，是 You're good. 說別人越來越好，是 *You're getting better.* 源自 You're getting better and better. 意思是「你們越來越好。」(詳見「文法寶典」p.202) 也可說成 You're improving. 〔ɪm'pruvɪŋ〕*v.* 改善；進步

【比較】 下面兩句話意義不同：

> *You're getting better.* (你們越來越好。)
> You're doing better.
> (你們現在表現得比較好。)
> 【這句話是 You're doing better now than you did before. 的省略】

下面的句子，我們按照美國老師使用的頻率排列：

① *You're getting better.*【第一常用】
   (你們越來越好。)
② You're getting much better.【第二常用】
   (你們現在好很多了。)
③ You're really getting much better.【第三常用】
   (你們現在眞的好很多了。)

12

④ You're really getting better.
   (你們眞的越來越好了。)
⑤ You're getting better each time.
   (你們一次比一次更好。)
⑥ You're getting better each day.
   (你們每天都越來越好。)

⑦ You're getting better every single day.

（你們每一天都越來越好。） 〔'sɪŋḷ〕*adj.* 單一的

⑧ You're all getting better.

（你們全都越來越好。）

⑨ You're all getting a lot better.

（你們都好很多了。）

⑩ You're all getting better and better.

（你們都變得越來越好了。）

5. *You're making progress.*

progress〔'prɑgrɛs , 'pro-〕*n.* 進步

make progress 進步

這句話的意思是「你們越來越進步了。」此句用現在進行式，既表「稱讚」，也表「越來越」，（詳見「文法寶典」p.342）。這句話和 You're getting better. 意義相同。

【比較1】 下面三句話意義不同：

You're making progress.（你們越來越進步了。）

You've made progress.（你們已經進步了。）

You made progress.（你們進步了。）

【比較2】 下面兩句話意思相同：

You're making progress.【通俗，一般語氣】

You're progressing.

【有一點咬文嚼字的味道，有學問的人喜歡說。

progress〔prə'grɛs〕*v.* 進步】

12

6. *You're on the right track.*

track〔 træk 〕 *n.* 軌道

on the right track 方向正確；做法、想法正確

　　track 的主要意思是「軌道」，一般是指「火車軌道」(= *train track*)。因為美國人早期，內陸交通工具以火車為主，從東岸到西岸大約三千英哩，都坐火車，所以，和 track 有關的成語和慣用語很多。

　　You're on the right track. 的字面意思是「你們在正確的軌道上。」引申為「你們方向正確；你們的做法正確；你們的想法正確。」

中文：你們方向正確。

英文：*You're on the right track.* 【第一常用】

= You're on the right road. 【第二常用】

= You're on the right path. 【第三常用】
　　　　　　　　　〔 pæθ 〕 *n.* 路徑

= You're going the right way. 【第六常用】

= You're taking the right path. 【第八常用】

= You're taking the right steps. 【常用】
　　　　　　　　　〔 stɛps 〕 *n. pl.* 步驟

= You're going on the right track. 【第七常用】

= You're heading in the right direction. 【第四常用】
　　　〔 'hɛdɪŋ 〕 *v.* 朝著

= You're heading the right way. 【第五常用】

12

【比較】 **You're on the right track.**
（你們方向正確；你們的做法正確。）
You're on the wrong track.
（你們方向錯誤；你們的做法錯誤。）

凡是你看到任何人，努力工作、有目標，你都可以說：**You're on the right track.** You're doing right.（你的方法正確。你做得對。）

7. *You make me proud.*

proud〔praʊd〕*adj.* 驕傲的；感到光榮的

這句話的字面意思是「你們使我感到驕傲。」引申為「我以你們為榮。」這句話等於 I'm proud of you.

下面是同類的說法，我們按照使用頻率排列：

① **You make me proud.**【第一常用】
（我以你們為榮。）
② I'm proud of you.【第二常用】
（我以你們為榮。）
③ I'm very proud of you.（我非常以你們為榮。）
④ I'm proud of your effort.
（我以你們的努力為榮。）
⑤ I'm proud of your work.
（我以你們的表現為榮。）
⑥ I'm proud of what you've done.
（我以你們所做的事為榮。）

12

8. ***You guys are the best.***

guy〔gaɪ〕*n.* 人

這句話的意思是「你們最棒。」guys 的用法，
詳見本書第三回。

下面稱讚的話，都是美國人喜歡說的，我們按
照使用頻率排列：

① ***You're the best.*** (你們最棒。)【第一常用】

② You're number one. (你們最好。)【第二常用】

③ You're the best of the best. (你們是最棒的。)

④ No one is better than you.
(沒有人比你們好。)

⑤ No one can compare to you.
〔kəm'pɛr〕*v.* 比較
(沒有人能和你們比。)
【在此 compare to = compare with】

⑥ Nobody is as good as you.
(沒有人像你們一樣好。)

下面是美國老師在課堂上常說的話：

You guys are the best. (你們是最棒的。)【第一常用】

You guys are the best students. 【第五常用】
(你們是最棒的學生。)

You guys are the best class. 【第四常用】
(你們是最棒的一班。)
【class 是指「全班同學」】

12

You guys really do the best.【第六常用】
（你們真的都盡力了。）
I think you guys are the very best.【第七常用】
（我認為你們棒極了。）
I think you guys are the very best class in
　　school.【第八常用】
（我認為你們就是全校最棒的一班。）
【very 是副詞，修飾形容詞 best，加強語氣】

You're the best students.【第三常用】
（你們是最棒的學生。）
You're the best class.【第二常用】
（你們是最棒的一班。）
I think you guys are the best class around.
（我認為你們是這裡最棒的一班。）【第九常用】
【around 是 around here 的省略】

9. *I want to thank you all.*

　　　這句話的意思是「我要謝謝大家。」句中的 all，
是指「大家」（= *everybody*）。

　　　下面的話，老師都可以在課堂上說，我們按照
使用頻率排列：

　　① *I want to thank you all.*【第一常用】
　　　　（我要謝謝大家。）
　　② I want to thank everybody.【第二常用】
　　　　（我要謝謝大家。）
　　③ I want to thank each one of you.【第三常用】
　　　　（我要謝謝你們每一位。）

12

④ I want to thank every student here.
（我要謝謝在場的每位學生。）

⑤ I want to thank each and every student here.
（我要謝謝在場的每一位學生。）

⑥ I want to thank you all for the wonderful
class today.
（我要謝謝大家，你們今天上課表現得都很棒。）

⑦ I want to thank you for the great class.
（我要謝謝大家，你們上課表現得很棒。）

⑧ I want to thank you for the great effort.
（我要謝謝大家，你們非常努力。）

⑨ I want to thank you for the hard work.
（我要謝謝大家，你們非常努力。）

上面的句子中的 I want to 都可改成 I'd like
to。一般中國人都不習慣說 I want to thank you.
之類的話，但美國人常說。

「教師一口氣英語」的設計，是讓老師全程
都用英文上課，先背熟這 108 句以後，再隨時複
習這本書，就可以創造自己想說的任何句子。

12

【 對話練習 1 】

A：Great work today.

B：Thanks for the praise.
　　Thank you for the compliment.
　　It's kind of you to say so.
　　〖praise〔prez〕*n.* 讚美
　　　compliment〔ˈkɑmpləmənt〕*n.* 稱讚〗

A：你們今天表現得很好。

B：謝謝你的讚美。
　　謝謝你的稱讚。
　　你這麼說，人真好。

A：Great effort, everybody.

B：Thanks for saying that.
　　We appreciate hearing that.
　　　　〔əˈpriʃɪˌet〕*v.* 感激

　　We're glad you're satisfied.

A：你們很努力。

B：謝謝你這麼說。
　　我們聽你這麼說，十分
　　感激。
　　我們很高興能讓你滿意。

A：You did a super job.

B：You're kind to say so.
　　I hope it's true.
　　I'm really trying hard.

A：你表現得太棒了。

B：你這麼說，人真好。
　　我希望這是真的。
　　我真的很努力。

A：You're getting better.

B：Thanks for the kind word.
　　I hope you're right.
　　I really want to improve.

A：你越來越好了。

B：謝謝你說這麼體貼的話。
　　我希望你說得沒錯。
　　我真的很想進步。

12

【對話練習 2】

A：You're making progress.

B：Thanks for noticing.
　　I can feel it.
　　It's a great feeling.

A：You're on the right track.

B：That's good to know.
　　That makes me feel better.
　　Sometimes I'm not so sure.

A：You make me proud.

B：You flatter me!
　　What a nice thing to say!
　　I feel the same way about
　　you.

【flatter (ˈflætɚ) v. 使受寵若驚；奉承】

12

A：You guys are the best.

B：It's because of you.
　　You're the reason why.
　　You are really the best.

A：你越來越進步了。

B：謝謝你注意到了。
　　我可以感覺得到。
　　這種感覺很棒。

A：你的做法正確。

B：知道這一點，真是太好了。
　　那讓我覺得好多了。
　　我有時候會不太確定。

A：我以你為榮。

B：我真是受寵若驚！
　　這麼說真好！
　　我對你也有同樣的感覺。

A：你們是最棒的。

B：那都是因為你。
　　那都是因為你。
　　你真的是最棒的。

「教師一口氣英語」經

唸英文要像唸經一樣，每天大聲唸，從起床到睡覺，唸得比看得快，最後不看也會唸，養成習慣後，你會全身舒爽，你試試看，奇妙無比。

1. Listen up, class.
   Let's get started.
   Let's get to work.

   We have lots to do.
   We have no time to waste.
   We're going full speed ahead.

   Aim high.
   Shoot for the stars.
   Let's have a great class today.

2. Follow me.
   Repeat after me.
   Repeat exactly what I say.

   Say what I say.
   Do what I do.
   All eyes on me.

   Raise your hand.
   Make a fist.
   Sound off after me.

3. Louder, please.
   Speak up, guys.
   Say it loud and clear.

   Raise your voices.
   I can't hear you.
   Don't sound like zombies.

   Turn it up.
   Shout it out!
   Tell it to the world!

4. *Read* aloud.
   Read in unison.
   Read all together as one.

   I'll say the first line.
   You repeat and continue.
   Go on and on nonstop.

   Don't let up.
   Keep at it!
   Keep going no matter what.

5. *Time to* recite.
   Time to remember.
   Let's practice and rehearse.

   No books allowed.
   Rely on your memory.
   Show me what you know.

   Who volunteers?
   Who's first?
   You all must take a turn.

6. Go for *it!*
   Just do *it!*
   Give *it* a try.

   Give it a shot.
   You can do it.
   You have nothing to lose.

   Get up here.
   Get out of your seat.
   Come on up and try.

7. *Take* a break.
Take a rest.
Everybody take five.

Go get some air.
Go get a drink.
Stand up and stretch.

Don't be late.
Don't make me wait.
Please be back on time.

8. *Let's* continue.
Let's carry on.
Let's get back to work.

Look alive!
Snap to it!
Show some life.

Heads *up*.
Sit *up* straight.
Get those shoulders back.

9. Pay attention.
Settle down.
Let's behave.

Stop the chatter.
No talking whatsoever.
No fooling or goofing around.

We're a team.
We're working together.
We're here to accomplish big things.

10. *Write* out the lesson.
Write it from memory.
Write it down word for word.

Make sure you print.
Make it look neat.
Don't scribble.

Take your time.
Get it right.
Do a good job.

11. Time's up.
That's it for now.
That's all for today.

Class is over.
Class dismissed.
Don't forget your assignment.

Memorize the lesson.
Learn it by heart.
Be ready for a quiz.

12. *Great* work today.
Great effort, everybody.
You did a super job.

You're getting better.
You're making progress.
You're on the right track.

You make me proud.
You guys are the best.
I want to thank you all.

14. 課堂上插入語

Five seconds to speak.
Nine lines to succeed.
One Breath English is the way.

Just open your mouth.
Take a deep breath.
Let it all hang out.

Learn it once.
Remember it forever.
Speak great English for life.

---

second (ˈsɛkənd)　　　　line (laɪn)
breath (brɛθ)　　　　　way (we)
mouth (mauθ)　　　　　*take a deep breath*
hang out　　　　　　　*let it all hang out*
once (wʌns)　　　　　　*for life*

【內文解説】

Five seconds to speak.	你只有五秒鐘的時間說。
Nine lines to succeed.	你必須說九句，才會成功。
One Breath English is the way.	「一口氣英語」是唯一的方法。
Just open your mouth.	只要把嘴巴張開。
Take a deep breath.	做個深呼吸。
Let it all hang out.	把它全部說出來。
Learn it once.	只要學一次。
Remember it forever.	就永遠記得。
Speak great English for life.	一輩子都會說很棒的英語。

** ――――――――――――

second〔'sɛkənd〕*n.* 秒　　line〔laɪn〕*n.* 行；短句

breath〔brɛθ〕*n.* 呼吸　　way〔we〕*n.* 方法

mouth〔mauθ〕*n.* 嘴巴　　***take a deep breath*** 做個深呼吸

hang out 掛出來；閒蕩

let it all hang out 把它全部說出來

once〔wʌns〕*adv.* 一次

for life 終生（ = *for the rest of your life* ）

14

【背景説明】

　　老師上課的時候，可隨時説一些鼓勵同學的話。這一回只是個例子，在「劉毅演講式英語」中，有很多内容可以引用。學生在課堂上吶喊多了，老師就可講這九句話，讓學生稍爲休息一下。

1. *Five seconds to speak.*
second〔'sɛkənd〕*n.* 秒

　　源自：You must speak it in five seconds.（你必須在五秒鐘之內把它說完。）強調「你只有五秒鐘。」（*You only have five seconds.*）這句話引申的意思是：「你只有五秒鐘的時間說。」

2. *Nine lines to succeed.*
line〔laɪn〕*n.* 行；短句
succeed〔sək'sid〕*v.* 成功

　　源自：You have to say nine lines to succeed.（你必須說九句，才會成功。）在「一口氣英語」中，每一句就是一行，美國人習慣把這種短句稱作 line。

　　這句話字面的意思是「九句話就會成功。」引申爲「如果你說九句，你就會成功。」（= *Say nine lines, and you'll succeed.*）也就是「你必須說九句，才會成功。」

14

3. *One Breath English is the way.*

　　這句話字面的意思是「『一口氣英語』就是方法。」引申為「『一口氣英語』是唯一的方法。」也可以加強語氣說成：*One Breath English* is the only way. (「一口氣英語」是唯一的方法。) 或 *One Breath English* is the best way. (「一口氣英語」是最好的方法。)

4. *Let it all hang out.*

　　hang out 掛在外面；閒蕩

　　這句話的字面意思是「讓它全部掛在外面。」hang out 這個成語的用法，在「一口氣英語⑤」p.12-8 中，有詳細的說明。***Let it all hang out.*** 是一個慣用句，美國人很常說，一般英漢字典都找不到這句話，要看實際情況，來決定它的意思，主要的意思是「把它全部說出來。」或「盡全力。」

【例1】 What's the matter? (有什麼不對？)
　　　　You can tell me. (你可以告訴我。)
　　　　Let it all hang out. (把它全部說出來。)

此時 Let it all hang out. 意思是「全部說出來，毫無保留。」(= *Tell everything and hold back nothing.*)

14

【例2】　Go for it. (趕快去做。)

Just do it. (去做吧。)

Let it all hang out. (盡全力。)

此時，Let it all hang out. 的意思是「盡全力。」
(= *Give it your best effort.*)

在運動的時候，美國人常說：

Go for broke. (盡全力。)
【詳見「劉毅演講式英語①」p.1-24】

Give it a try. (試一試。)

Let it all hang out. (盡全力。)

美國老師叫學生說實話，也常說：

Be honest. (要誠實。)

Tell the truth. (說實話。)

Let it all hang out. (全部說出來。)

老師第一次上課英語演講稿

　　老師第一天上課，給學生的第一印象最重要，教「一口氣英語」時，先用英語發表一次演講，上課前，一定要背得滾瓜爛熟，講的時候才有信心。說話速度儘量慢，但是要有力量。

15. *What Is One Breath English?*

Dear ladies and gentlemen:
Thank you for the warm welcome.
It's an honor to be here today.

I'm here on a mission.
I have an important message.
I'm convinced it will change your life.

English is everywhere.
English is a key to success.
We must learn and master it.

---

warm〔wɔrm〕 honor〔'ɑnɚ〕
mission〔'mɪʃən〕 message〔'mɛsɪdʒ〕
convinced〔kən'vɪnst〕 key〔ki〕
master〔'mæstɚ〕

15

So many of us study English like hell.
So few of us can speak it well.
What do you think is the reason?

The problem is right here! (*Point to your brain*)
The problem is remembering.
The problem is that we forget what we learn.

Luckily, through years of research, we've created a new way to learn.
With this specially designed material and method, we can retain what we learn forever.
It's called *One Breath English.*

---

like hell	brain〔bren〕
through〔θru〕	research〔'risɜtʃ〕
create〔krɪ'et〕	design〔dɪ'zaɪn〕
material〔mə'tɪrɪəl〕	method〔'mɛθəd〕
retain〔rɪ'ten〕	

15

What is *One Breath English*?
Why should we learn it?
What's it all about?

First, it's a breakthrough technique.
It's easy to remember.
It's designed to be memorized.

Repeat nine lines like crazy.
Speak as fast as you can.
Say it within five seconds.

It will become second nature.
It will be ingrained in your memory.
You will remember it for the rest of
　　your life.

---

breakthrough (ˈbrekˌθru)　　technique (tɛkˈnik)
memorize (ˈmɛməˌraɪz)　　repeat (rɪˈpit)
line (laɪn)　　*like crazy*
within (wɪðˈɪn)　　second (ˈsɛkənd)
second nature　　ingrained (ɪnˈgrend)
memory (ˈmɛmərɪ)　　rest (rɛst)

15

Second, the material is full of life.
It's not boring book English.
It's the core essence of daily
   American speech.

The content is uplifting.
It's considerate and polite.
People will like what you say.

You'll gain confidence.
You'll communicate better.
You'll become a better person.

---

be full of
core〔kor〕
daily〔'delɪ〕
content〔'kɑntɛnt〕
considerate〔kən'sɪdərɪt〕
confidence〔'kɑnfədəns〕
communicate〔kə'mjunəˌket〕

boring〔'borɪŋ〕
essence〔'ɛsns̩〕
speech〔spitʃ〕
uplifting〔ʌp'lɪftɪŋ〕
gain〔gen〕

15

Third, it's fun to learn.
It's a five second test.
It's just like playing a game.

You challenge yourself.
You race against the clock.
You will improve every time you try.

Speak English to yourself day
and night.
Speak English to everyone
around you.
It's fun to impress people.

---

fun〔 fʌn 〕	challenge〔'tʃælɪndʒ 〕
race against	*race against the clock*
improve〔 ɪm'pruv 〕	*speak to oneself*
day and night	impress〔 ɪm'prɛs 〕

15

Fourth, One Breath English is very healthy.
It's a fountain of youth.
It will make you become younger.

What makes people grow old?
It's anxiety, stress and loss of hope.
Reciting English will cure these problems.

Chant *it* over and over.
Say *it* to yourself again and again.
Your anxiety, depression, and loneliness
   will all go away.

---

healthy (ˈhɛlθɪ)   fountain (ˈfaʊntn̩)
youth (juθ)   grow (gro)
anxiety (æŋˈzaɪətɪ)   stress (strɛs)
loss (lɔs)   recite (rɪˈsaɪt)
cure (kjʊr)   chant (tʃænt)
over and over   *say to* oneself
again and again   depression (dɪˈprɛʃən)
loneliness (ˈlonlɪnɪs)   *go away*

15

The bottom line is that One Breath
　English gets results.
It's organized and systematic.
It's efficient learning right away.

This is a great discovery.
It's totally revolutionary.
It's unprecedented in language learning
　history.

The English revolution is NOW!
One Breath English is the way.
Let's open our books and begin.

---

bottom line	result〔rɪ'zʌlt〕
organized〔'ɔrgən,aɪzd〕	
systematic〔,sɪstə'mætɪk〕	
efficient〔ə'fɪʃənt〕	***right away***
discovery〔dɪ'skʌvərɪ〕	totally〔'totl̩ɪ〕
revolutionary〔,rɛvə'luʃən,ɛrɪ〕	
unprecedented〔ʌn'prɛsə,dɛntɪd〕	
revolution〔,rɛvə'luʃən〕	way〔we〕

15

15. *What Is One Breath English?*
什麼是「一口氣英語」?

Dear ladies and gentlemen:	各位親愛的先生、女士:
Thank you for the warm welcome.	謝謝你們熱烈的歡迎。
It's an honor to be here today.	很榮幸今天能來到這裡。
***I*'m here on a mission.**	我來這裡有個使命。
***I* have an important message.**	我有個重要的訊息。
***I*'m convinced it will change your life.**	我相信它會改變你的一生。
***English* is everywhere.**	英文無所不在。
***English* is a key to success.**	英文是成功的關鍵。
We must learn and master it.	我們必須學習並精通英文。

** ────────────────

warm〔wɔrm〕*adj.* 親切的　　honor〔'ɑnɚ〕*n.* 光榮
mission〔'mɪʃən〕*n.* 任務;使命
message〔'mɛsɪdʒ〕*n.* 訊息
convinced〔kən'vɪnst〕*adj.* 確信的
key〔ki〕*n.* 關鍵 <*to*>　　master〔'mæstɚ〕*v.* 精通

15

So many of us study English like hell.

我們有很多人拼命地學英文。

So few of us can speak it well.

卻很少有人能把英文說得很好。

What do you think is the reason?

你們認爲原因是什麼？

The problem is right here! (*Point to your brain*)

問題就在這裡！
（手指著腦袋）

The problem is remembering.

問題就在於記憶。

The problem is that we forget what we learn.

問題在於，我們會忘記學過的東西。

Luckily, through years of research, we've created a new way to learn.

幸運的是，經過多年的研究，我們已經創造出一個新的學習方法。

With this specially designed material and method, we can retain what we learn forever.

有了這個特別設計的教材和方法，我們可以永遠記住所學過的東西。

It's called *One Breath English*.

它就叫「一口氣英語」。

**

like hell 拼命地　　brain〔 bren 〕*n.* 頭腦
luckily〔ˈlʌkɪlɪ〕*adv.* 幸運地　　through〔 θru 〕*prep.* 經過
research〔ˈrisɝtʃ〕*n.* 研究　　create〔 krɪˈet 〕*v.* 創造
design〔 dɪˈzaɪn 〕*v.* 設計　　material〔 məˈtɪrɪəl 〕*n.* 材料；教材
method〔ˈmɛθəd〕*n.* 方法　　retain〔 rɪˈten 〕*v.* 保留；記住

15

What is *One Breath English*?	什麼是「一口氣英語」？
Why should we learn it?	爲什麼我們應該學習它？
What's it all about?	它到底是怎麼回事？
First, it's a breakthrough technique.	首先，它是個突破性的方法。
It's easy to remember.	它很容易記。
It's designed to be memorized.	它是爲了讓人背得下來而設計的。
Repeat nine lines like crazy.	拼命地重覆唸九句。
Speak as fast as you can.	儘可能快速地唸。
Say it within five seconds.	唸到五秒鐘之內。
It will become second nature.	它就會成爲你的本能。
It will be ingrained in your memory.	它將會深植於你的記憶中。
You will remember it for the rest of your life.	你終生都不會忘記。

** ————————————————

breakthrough〔'brek,θru〕*n.* 突破
technique〔tɛk'nik〕*n.* 技術；方法
memorize〔'mɛmə,raɪz〕*v.* 記住　　repeat〔rɪ'pit〕*v.* 重複
like crazy 拼命地　　within〔wɪð'ɪn〕*prep.* 在…之內
second〔'sɛkənd〕*n.* 秒
second nature 與生俱來的本能；第二天性
ingrained〔ɪn'grend〕*adj.* 根深蒂固的

15

***Second*, *the material is full of life*.**	第二，它的資料充滿了生命。
It's not boring book English.	它並非無聊的書本英語。
It's the core essence of daily American speech.	它是美國日常生活會話精華中的精華。
The content is uplifting.	它的內容振奮人心。
It's considerate and polite.	它既體貼又有禮貌。
People will like what you say.	人們會喜歡你所說的話。
You'll gain confidence.	你會增加信心。
You'll communicate better.	你會更容易跟人溝通。
You'll become a better person.	你會成為更好的人。

**─────────────────────

be full of 充滿　　boring〔'borɪŋ〕*adj.* 無聊的
core〔kor〕*n.* 核心；精髓　　essence〔'ɛsn̩s〕*n.* 精髓；要素
daily〔'delɪ〕*adj.* 日常的　　speech〔spitʃ〕*n.* 說話；會話
content〔'kɑntɛnt〕*n.* 內容
uplifting〔ʌp'lɪftɪŋ〕*adj.* 鼓舞人心的
considerate〔kən'sɪdərɪt〕*adj.* 體貼的
gain〔gen〕*v.* 獲得；增加
confidence〔'kɑnfədəns〕*n.* 信心
communicate〔kə'mjunə,ket〕*v.* 溝通

15

Third, ***it's fun to learn***.	第三，它學起來很有趣。
It's a five second test.	它是個五秒鐘的測試。
It's just like playing a game.	它就像是在玩遊戲。
You challenge yourself.	你挑戰自己。
You race against the clock.	你和時間賽跑。
You will improve every time you try.	你每次嘗試都會有進步。
Speak English to yourself day and night.	要日夜不停地自言自語說英文。
Speak English to everyone around you.	對身旁的每個人說英文。
It's fun to impress people.	讓人佩服很有趣。

** ————————————————

fun〔fʌn〕*adj.* 好玩的　　challenge〔'tʃælɪndʒ〕*v.* 挑戰
race against 和…賽跑
race against the clock 和時鐘賽跑；和時間賽跑
improve〔ɪm'pruv〕*v.* 改善；進步
speak to *oneself* 自言自語　　***day and night*** 日夜不停地
impress〔ɪm'prɛs〕*v.* 使印象深刻；使佩服

15

Fourth**, **One Breath English is
　***very healthy**.*
It's a fountain of youth.
It will make you become younger.

What makes people grow old?
It's anxiety, stress and loss of
　hope.
Reciting English will cure these
　problems.

Chant *it* over and over.
Say *it* to yourself again and again.
Your anxiety, depression, and
　loneliness will all go away.

第四，「一口氣英語」十
分有益健康。
它是青春之泉。
它會使你變得更年輕。

人為什麼會變老？
是因為焦慮、壓力，和
失去希望。
背誦英文能治好這些問
題。

要反覆不停地說。
要不斷地自言自語。
你的焦慮、沮喪和寂寞，
都會消失。

** ─────────────────

healthy〔'hɛlθɪ〕*adj.* 健康的　　fountain〔'faʊntn̩〕*n.* 泉源
youth〔juθ〕*n.* 年輕　　grow〔gro〕*v.* 變得
anxiety〔æŋ'zaɪətɪ〕*n.* 焦慮　　stress〔strɛs〕*n.* 壓力
loss〔lɔs〕*n.* 失去　　recite〔rɪ'saɪt〕*v.* 背誦
cure〔kjʊr〕*v.* 治好；消除　　chant〔tʃænt〕*v.* 吟唱；反覆說
over and over 一再地（= *again and again*）
say to *oneself* 自言自語　　depression〔dɪ'prɛʃən〕*n.* 沮喪
loneliness〔'lonlɪnɪs〕*n.* 寂寞　　***go away*** 離開；消失

15

The bottome line is that One Breath English gets results.
It's organized and systematic.
It's efficient learning right away.

最重要的是,「一口氣英語」有效果。
它有條理,而且有系統。
學了立刻有效果。

This is a great discovery.
It's totally revolutionary.
It's unprecedented in language learning history.

這是一項偉大的發現。
它完全是革命性的。
它是語言學習史上史無前例的創舉。

The English revolution is NOW!
One Breath English is the way.

英語革命就在現在!
「一口氣英語」是唯一的方法。

Let's open our books and begin.

我們把書打開,開始上課吧。

** ——————————————

bottom line 要點;主要考慮
result〔rɪ'zʌlt〕*n.* 成果;效果
organized〔'ɔrgən‚aɪzd〕*adj.* 有組織的;有條理的
systematic〔‚sɪstə'mætɪk〕*adj.* 有系統的
efficient〔ə'fɪʃənt〕*adj.* 有效率的　　***right away*** 立刻
discovery〔dɪ'skʌvərɪ〕*n.* 發現　　totally〔'totl̩ɪ〕*adv.* 完全地
revolutionary〔‚rɛvə'luʃən‚ɛrɪ〕*adj.* 革命性的
unprecedented〔ʌn'prɛsə‚dɛntɪd〕*adj.* 空前的;史無前例的
revolution〔‚rɛvə'luʃən〕*n.* 革命　　way〔we〕*n.* 方法

15

【背景説明】

　　這篇演講稿，是介紹「一口氣英語」，專門設計給老師第一堂上課使用。老師每一堂上課，最好都先用英文發表一次演講。

1. ***I'm convinced it will change your life.***
   convince〔kən'vɪns〕*v.* 使確信；使相信

   　　convince 這個字很特別，「使某人相信某事」，就是 convince *sb.* of *sth.* ，「自己相信某事」就是 convince *oneself* of *sth.* 它的被動態就是 be convinced of *sth.* ，接 that 子句的時候，介系詞 of 必須省略，that 可以省略或保留。

   　　I'm convince (that) it will change your life.
   = I'm sure it will change your life.

2. ***What's it all about?***

   　　這句話的字面意思是「它全部是關於什麼的？」引申為「它到底是怎麼回事？」也可以說成：What's this all about? 或 What on earth is this all about? (它到底究竟是怎麼回事？)

3. ***It's the core essence of daily American speech.***
   core〔kor〕*n.* 核心；精髓　　essence〔'ɛsns〕*n.* 精髓
   speech〔spitʃ〕*n.* 談話 (= *conversation* = *dialogue*)

   　　core 和 essence 這兩個字意思相同，在這裡是名詞修飾名詞，core essence 是指「精華中的精

華」，speech 在此不是指「演講」，是指日常生活
中的「會話」。整句話的意思是「它是美國日常生
活會話精華中的精華。」

4. *It will become second nature.*

　　second nature 字典上大多翻成「第二天性」，
但是中國人不這麼説。應該翻成「與生俱來的本
能」。這句話的意思是「它將成為你的本能。」
(= *It will seem like you were born with it.*)

5. *Chant it over and over.*
　 Say it again and again.
　 chant〔tʃænt〕*v.* 吟唱；反覆説
　 over and over　一再地 (= *again and again*)

　　這兩句話的意思是「要反覆不停地説。」凡是
一個人在自言自語説同樣的話，都可以説是 Chant
it over and over. 或 Say it again and again.

6. *It's efficient learning right away.*
　 efficient〔ə'fɪʃənt〕*adj.* 有效率的
　 right away　立刻

　　這句話字面的意思是「它是立刻有效率的學習。」
所謂「有效率的學習」(efficient learning)，就是
get results，所以可引申為「學了有效」，這句話
的英文解釋是：You get results without wasting
time right away.

INDEX

索引

索引

索引

索引

索引

索引

索引

索引

索引

索引

索引

索引

索引

劉 毅老師 徵訓
「一口氣英語」種子老師

1. 35歲以下，身強力壯，聲音宏亮。
2. 能夠一分鐘內背完本書十二回108句。
3. 對「一口氣英語」教學有興趣。
4. 能夠站在椅子上或桌子上，帶領同學吶喊，激起同學瘋狂地背「一口氣英語」。
5. 願意接受最嚴格的訓練。
6. 願意出差到任何地方，大陸或國外，推廣「一口氣英語」。
7. 前三個月訓練期間，底薪5萬元，訓練後，表現優良，薪資沒有上限。
8. 面試地點：台北市重慶南路一段10號7樓（週一至週五，下午3:00～10:00，週六、週日及例假日，全天開放。）

早上起來，

一面散步，一面背

「一口氣英語」，

快樂無比。

每一回

一定要背到5秒鐘之內，

否則早晚會忘記。

養成自言自語說英文的習慣，

英文進步神速，

每天都有成就感。

有了「一口氣英語」，

學說英語並不是什麼困難的事，

只要不停地鍛鍊，

誰都會說英文。